BACK FROM HELL . . .

The old man stared down at his dead brother, and his rheumy eyes filled with tears.

"The chief, he say to me, 'Tell the soldiers that Narbona was here. You tell them or I will come back and cut your throat.' That is what he say, this chief, this filth of a man."

"Narbona?" Zak said, so soft the old man could barely hear him. "There was a Narbona once, a Navajo warrior, a very bad man. A thief. A killer. A man without mercy. That Narbona has been dead a long time."

It was odd. When a Navajo died, his name was never mentioned again. Nor was it ever used again by any living Navajo.

The Navajo had not tried to hide their tracks. They had openly murdered a poor farmer, left him on the road in plain sight.

This did not look like anything Zak had seen before . . .

By Jory Sherman

Shadow Rider

BLOOD SKY AT MORNING
APACHE SUNDOWN
GHOST WARRIOR

THE BARON HONOR
BLOOD RIVER
THE VIGILANTE
TEXAS DUST
THE BARON WAR
THE BRAZOS
ABILENE GUN DOWN
THE SOUTH PLATTE
VISIONS OF A LOST GIRL
CHILL #1: SATAN'S SEED
CHILL #2: SEPULCHRE

SHADOW RIDER

GHOST WARRIOR

JORY SHERMAN

wm

WILLIAM MORROW
An Imprint of HarperCollinsPublishers

SHADOW RIDER: GHOST WARRIOR. Copyright © 2008 by Jory Sherman. All rights reserved. Printed in the United States of America. No part of this book may be used or reproduced in any manner whatsoever without written permission except in the case of brief quotations embodied in critical articles and reviews. For information, address HarperCollins Publishers, 195 Broadway, New York, NY 10007.

First William Morrow mass market printing: December 2018
First Harper mass market printing: July 2008

Print Edition ISBN: 978-0-06-088530-4
Digital Edition ISBN: 978-0-06-198342-9

Cover design by Nadine Badalaty
Cover illustration by Ken Laegar

William Morrow and HarperCollins are registered trademarks of HarperCollins Publishers in the United States of America and other countries.

18 19 20 21 22   QGM   10 9 8 7 6 5 4 3 2

To the memory of my friend,
Raymond Friday Locke,
who wrote the book on the Navajo

SHADOW RIDER

GHOST WARRIOR

1

Zak Cody could smell death the way some men can smell perfume on a woman. He had sniffed both in his life, and sometimes both spelled trouble.

Now he rode through the long shadows of afternoon, a shadow among shadows, following the tracks of unshod ponies, tracks he read like words in a book, like cloud tracings in the sky, like footprints in virgin snow.

Eight ponies, he counted, by their spoor. Eight ponies carrying Navajo warriors who should have been tending corn on a reservation. But that was not the worst of it.

Eight Navajo ponies, yes. But also two shod horses, bringing the rider count to ten strong.

And the mounts wearing iron shoes had not been in the bunch when Zak had started tracking.

Near as he could figure, those two extra horses joined the Navajos sometime during the night before.

And they had come from the east, from the direction of Santa Fe. To Zak, that meant only one thing.

White men.

Two white men and eight Navajo.

The mix could mean only one thing.

Trouble.

Big trouble.

He did not like where the tracks were leading him, nor did he like the numbers of them, the story they told—of renegade Navajo braves on a mission to some place along the Rio Grande—*El Rio Grande del Norte*, the Mexicans called it—a river that rose in the Rocky Mountains in Colorado, and ran all the way to Texas and Mexico before joining the even bigger waters of the Gulf.

These Navajos knew where they were going, and from the scent in the air that afternoon, they had already gotten to that place.

A place of death.

The hills behind him and the Jemez Mountains, rising up like great ships on a misty sea, basked in lavender shadows, as if resting from a day of molten sun. Along the river the breeze flitted among the cottonwoods, whose leaves shimmied like the spangles on a glitter gal's slinky dress, and doves flew north along the watery highway, their bodies twisting in unison, their delicate gray wings whistling tuneless, disconnected notes in a minor key.

The tracks were hours old. Half a day had gone by since he started reading them out of a swirl surrounding a lone *carreta*, where a slaughtered burro lay dead in its traces. The driver was a bloody pile of rags atop the box he had used for a seat, a bullet hole in his chest and his throat slashed to a gaping grin, clear to the spine. One savage swipe, and the blood had gushed out of the man's chest as if someone had emptied a can of barn paint onto his dusty white shirt.

The buzzards had drawn Zak to that place. He had seen them spiraling in the sky on their airy carousels, flapping in from the mountains and the desert. None had yet landed, or the farmer's eyes would have been plucked out like black olives from a jar. The man's flesh had not yet been shredded and there was still warmth on his belly and under his armpits. Dead maybe a half hour, Zak had figured. He should have sighted the Navajos not long after, but his horse had stumbled on a rock and grazed his leg on some cholla. It had taken Zak better than an hour to remove the delicate hairs and rub salve on the tiny holes in the gelding's ankle and hock.

The Navajos had eaten some of the tomatoes and beans the *campesino* was taking to market in his cart. They had ransacked the wagon, leaving the uncovered boxes of vegetables to rot in the sun as they rode on to the south. Three hours ago the Navajos had met up with the two men on shod horses, stopped and smoked, pissed, squatted, and set out on a steady course that followed a deep dry creek bed running parallel to the river. Ten men, low and out of sight from anyone passing on the road. He had seen where they all had stopped there, lay their horses down for a time. Turning invisible to any but the most observant. Bedded down and waited, not wanting to be seen.

The white men left traces of cigarette paper and burnt tobacco along their path. Papers clinging to prickly-pear spines and crushed under overturned pebbles, buried under boot heels, stubbed down by toes pressing on hard narrow soles, left tattered and dirty with sand and grit as if in testimony to their passing. The cigarettes were store-bought, filled with prime Virginia latakia, cured to a sunburnt gold. Moneyed men, he figured, and wondered what he was up against on a mission delegated to him by none other than his friend General George C. Crook.

Zak had the letter in his pocket, folded neatly and encased in oilcloth. The order directed him to proceed to Taos and investigate suspicious predations along the Rio Grande. As usual, his orders were secret and not to be revealed to any person unless absolutely necessary. It was addressed to him by his military title, Colonel Zak Cody. Zak was a civilian, but he was also still in the military, answerable only to Crook and President U.S. Grant.

Zak felt the heat of the blazing sun through the cloth of his black shirt and black trousers. Even his hat was black. His horse, too. His horse was named Nox, the Latin word for "night," and it was a fitting name for the gelding, whose sleek hide glistened in the sun, like polished ebony or black teak.

There was a cottony sea of sheep grazing on the other side of the river, the herders, with crooked staffs, walking slowly along its edge. Little black-and-white dogs kept the herd together, running back and forth, then sprawling flat with their front paws outstretched like matching andirons, their heads still, but their eyes watching every move of the sheep in their charge.

Then he ran into more sheep on his side of the river, and saw the adobe huts and the gardens with the knee-high corn and bean stakes and red peppers dangling among the green like miniature piñatas.

And no dogs and no sheepherders that he could see.

Zak loosened the Winchester '73 in its boot and lifted the Colt from its holster so that it was not seated so tight. His eyes glittered as they narrowed and he watched Nox's ears twist into hard cones and stiffen as they tipped forward to catch any alien sound. The Colt was new, a Peacemaker, in .45 caliber, much lighter than the converted Walker he used to carry.

Flies flew at Nox, whose switching tail swept them aside, and those that escaped darted at Zak's head and pestered Nox's ears. Their buzzing made the adobe buildings seem even more silent as he passed near them, heading toward a larger one sitting on a small green hill covered with an irrigated grass carpet. Flowers bordered the house and stood in pots on window ledges, red and purple and yellow, the petals in full bloom.

Zak's gut tightened as he approached the house and saw the dead dog lying on the path that led to the front door. The door gaped open. He saw something flutter just inside, a scrap of cloth, pale blue with a strip of red and yellow symbols running through it.

"Hello, the house," Zak called, and his voice sounded hollow to him.

There was no answer.

"*Hola, la casa,*" he called in Spanish as he reined in Nox at a hitchrail some yards from the dwelling.

He sat there for a moment, listening. Nox's ears twisted in a half arc, back and forth. His rubbery nostrils quivered as he tossed his head, trying to pick up some intelligible scent.

"Settle down, Nox," Zak said, his voice soft and low so that only he and his horse could hear the words. Nox responded, and the muscles in his shoulder stopped quivering.

He called out to the house again, and this time, he heard a low moan coming from inside. His temple pulsed with the increase of his heart rate, and he swung out of the saddle, his lean and supple body graceful as a dancer's in its precise and flowing movement.

He wrapped the reins around the weathered hitchrail, turning his head back and forth, his senses alert to any danger from around the adobe dwelling.

Zak drew his pistol and he stepped inside the house, crouching catlike to offer less of a target to anyone waiting in ambush.

"Hello," he crooned in his bass-timbred voice.

"*¡Ay de mí! Ayudarme.*"

He stood there, letting his eyes adjust to the dim light. He looked down, saw the woman's dress just to the right of his boots. She had not been the one to call out. She lay stiff and still, like a broken doll, and he thought she was dead.

Feeble light splayed through the windows, the beams caught in rods. Dust motes flickered in the shafts like ghostly fireflies, and he saw a sandaled foot in one of the parallelograms on the floor. He stepped toward it and saw the figure of a man sprawled on his back, a bullet hole in his sunken chest, his eyes wide open in a death stare, his mouth open in a silent scream.

Zak walked past him, satisfied that he, too, was

dead, and then heard a stirring from behind a rustic couch off to his left. He walked over to it and looked behind it.

"Can you stand up?" he asked in Spanish. "I will not hurt you."

He heard a groan and then saw two hands come up, grip the back of the couch. A second later an old man stood up. His arms shook as he released his grip on the couch. His white shirt was mottled with blood spatter. A red bandanna encircled his neck, and his eyes bulged from their sockets like a pair of billiard balls.

"Who are you?" Zak asked, in Spanish.

"*Soy un hombre muerto*," the man husked. I am a dead man.

2

Zak's jaw tightened as he looked at the frightened man. There was blood, thick, in his sideburns and an ugly mass of flesh on top of his head, as if he had been smashed with a claw hammer. His lips quivered and his hands shook. His eyes showed the fear that was in him, the fear an animal shows when it is wounded and knows it's about to die.

"You are not dead," Zak said.

The two men spoke only in Spanish.

"Are you not Death?"

Zak shook his head.

"I saw the black horse. You wear the black clothing. You have the appearance of Death."

"That is my way. I am a friend."

"A friend?"

"Yes. I rode by and saw the dead dog. What passed here, old man? Who are these dead on the floor?"

"They came. The Indians. And two white men. They killed my brother and his wife. They shot them. They beat me after they told me what to do when they were gone."

"They told you what to do after they were gone? And then they beat you?"

"My head hurts where the Indian, the leader, the chief, hit me until my blood poured over my face and the light went away. I thought I was dead. I thought you were Death. I thought the Indian sent Death back to take me to where my brother and my sister-in-law now are."

"Come, old man. Seat yourself. What are you called?"

The old man made his way around to the front of the moth-eaten couch and sat down gingerly. He sighed and touched fingers to the wound on top of his head. He winced with the sudden pain.

"I am called Gregorio Delacruz."

"You need not have fear. Tell me what the Indian chief told you."

Gregorio began to choke up. He stared down at his dead brother and his rheumy eyes filled with tears. Zak heard a rattling sound deep in the man's throat, as if his words were trapped there, mossed over like cold stones in a well.

"The chief, he say to me, 'Tell the soldiers. You go tell the soldiers. Tell the soldiers that Narbona was here. You tell them, or I will come back and cut your throat.' That is what he say, this chief, this filth of a man."

The columns of light began to dim, to weaken until they were as pale as faded buttercups. The geometrical patterns on the dirt floor began to lose definition and the shadows in the room deepened into inky masses. A chill crept into the room and some of the sheep began to bleat. Their pleading cries seemed to be disembodied, emerging from the earth like lost souls.

And the old man wept, holding his face in his hands as if to hide the shame of this weakness before another man.

Zak looked at the *bultos*, the little statues of saints, sunk into the adobe walls, the crucifix high above the fireplace, the sad wounded face of Jesus staring down at the weeping man. A clay statue of the Virgin Mary, robed in blue, stood on a small shelf in a corner, a votive candle, unlit, at her sandaled feet.

This was a deeply religious family, Zak thought, people of faith and hope, scratching a living from a harsh land, tending their sheep, selling the wool, caring for their lambs. And in a single day their world had been shattered, smashed, bloodied, and the one who had lived on was left wanting, frightened, broken on the wheel of life—by some men with a taste for blood.

"Narbona?" Zak said, so soft the old man could barely hear him.

"Yes, he told me that was what he was called. Narbona."

"There was a Narbona once, a Navajo warrior, who fought Kearney and Kit Carson. A very bad man. A thief. A killer. A man without mercy."

"I have heard of that man," Gregorio said. "But he is dead, is he not?"

Zak looked through the door at Nox, whose black form was swathed in shadow now, as the sun fell past the rim of the Jemez range. The sheep still bleated and there was nobody to tend them. The birds were flying to their night roosts and the land was beginning to gentle, as if smoothed by some unseen hand.

"Yes, that Narbona has been dead a long time," Zak said.

It was odd, he thought. When a Navajo died, his name was never mentioned again. Nor was it ever used again by any living Navajo.

"Did you hear the names of the white men? Or the names of any of the other Navajos?"

Gregorio raised his head. He swiped the sleeve of his shirt across his cheeks to erase his tears.

"I heard the name of 'Pete,' and the other one was called, how do you say it, 'Rafael'? No, a gringo—I mean, an American name."

"Ralph?" Zak said.

Gregorio nodded.

"Yes. Ralph. It is a difficult name to say on the Spanish tongue."

"What about the Indians? Hear any other names?"

"The one with Narbona, yes. Narbona called him Largos. That is an odd name, no?"

"Yes."

Largos, too, was a dead man's name. He had ridden with Narbona, fought against Kearney and Kit Carson when the government was trying to stop the stealing and the murders in New Mexico and drive the Indians to reservations. The Navajos had left a bloody trail, and it had taken years to isolate them. They had never been conquered, Zak thought, and now some of them were back on the rampage, murdering, pillaging, terrorizing settlers along the Rio Grande.

"Gregorio, do you want to wash your brother and dress him in clean clothes? And your brother's wife as well? I will help you bury them tomorrow."

"Yes. Help me carry them to their bed. I will wash and dress them."

"Where can I put up my horse? I will stay with you this night."

"There is a shed and a barn in back of this house. Did you not see it?"

"I was looking at other things," Zak said.

"Will Narbona come back this night?"

"No. Did he drive off any of your sheep? Did he steal anything, any of your stock?"

"I do not know. I heard the Indians yelling and cursing the sheep. I heard their guns. Maybe they killed some, or maybe they stole some of them. I do not know."

"Where are all the herders? All dead? Where are the children?"

"The children are in Santa Fe. They go to school. There was only one herder and me. I think they killed Juanito. I have not seen him."

"It will be dark soon. We can find out what I need to know in the morning."

Zak helped Gregorio carry the bodies of the dead woman and man into a back bedroom. There were three bedrooms, a small sewing room, and a kitchen. They laid the bodies on top of the bed, and Zak walked back outside to take care of Nox.

It was not yet dark, but the sun had fallen behind the mountains, leaving a pastel glow in the sky. Small, thin clouds hung like effigies of salmon or trout, their edges gleaming silver and gold against a paling aquamarine sky.

He found the small barn, put together with adobe and whipsawed lumber. There were two mules and a burro in it, and he found a bin of grain. He put Nox in a stall, stripped him of saddle, bridle, saddlebags, and rifle. He grained and watered all of the animals, left his saddle and bridle on a sawhorse near a small tack room. He carried his rifle and saddlebags back to the house and went inside. He closed the door and dropped the bar.

Gregorio had lit an oil lamp in the front room, and down the hall, Zak saw a pale orange light emanating from the back bedroom and some kind of yellow flickering light in the kitchen.

He took his rifle from its scabbard and leaned it against the wall by the front door. He set his saddlebags next to the couch and walked to the window to look out toward the river.

Zak's orders had been signed by an adjutant he did not know, a brevet colonel named Ernest Buehler, on behalf of General Crook. He wondered how much Crook knew about the "predations" along the Rio Grande. How long had they been going on? Did anyone know about a Navajo named Narbona? And what about Largos?

Perhaps those two were still alive. If they were, they would be very old. He would have to ask Gregorio about that.

Some odd thought scratched at a corner of his brain, clawed its way up out of the black morass of doubts and into the light of knowledge. What was going on? What was truly going on? Perhaps Crook did not know and meant for him to find out.

And why had Narbona told Gregorio to tell the soldiers that he had done these deeds?

Any other Indian raider would have tried to hide his tracks.

And who were the two white men with Narbona? Soldiers? Ex-soldiers? Deserters?

So many questions. And no answers.

The Navajos had not tried to hide their tracks. They had openly murdered a poor farmer, left him on the road in plain sight.

This did not look like anything Zak had seen before. In all of his years of fighting Indians with Crook and others, he had never encountered a puzzle of this complexity, an enigma that eluded explanation no matter how hard he looked at it, turned it around in his mind to examine all sides.

There was a chilling aspect to what Narbona had told Gregorio. "Go tell the soldiers," he had said.

Why? Zak wondered.

That was the last thing he would want if he were a hunted man—to have soldiers tracking him down.

Narbona wanted the soldiers to come after him. That was the only explanation Zak could come up with, and it didn't make sense.

"Why?" he asked again, this time out loud.

The land outside the window sank into shadow. He could see the flow of white sheep as they moved down to the river to drink, and they looked like foam on a long wave streaming across a dark sea. And off in the distance he heard a coyote call in the darkness, its voice a chromatic ribbon of melodious notes rising up the scale and hanging there until they faded into the empty cavern of a deep silence.

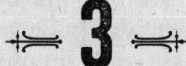

3

The stench of death clung to the walls of the adobe. Before dawn, while the dark was still upon the land, Zak arose from the bed Gregorio had given him and walked outside to breathe the still air, gaze at the stars, listen to the frogs down by the river, the murmurs of the sheep as they grumbled in their sleep.

He and Gregorio had eaten cold mutton, beans, and hard corn cakes the old man's sister-in-law had made. They talked of life and death, of injustice and prejudice.

"Democracy," Gregorio had said, "is a word found only in the dictionary. Discrimination is found everywhere."

Zak had not said anything, but he saw the truth in what Gregorio had said, from Gregorio's perspective. He learned that Gregorio and his brother, Pablo, had both been born in Socorro, had been raised dirt-poor, and had no education.

"You know what *socorro* means, eh?"

"I know," Zak said.

The word meant "help," or to be more precise, he thought, "succor."

"We had none in that little town," Gregorio said. "And my brother and I make a journey to Taos and then to Santa Fe. He met his wife, Consuela, in Santa Fe. Her father was poor and wanted to sell her so that his large family would have food."

"Your brother bought her?"

"Yes. He paid two dollars for her. It was all the money he had. I did not have money, so I could not buy Consuela's sister, Loreta. I did not like her anyway. She was ugly. She had the bad breath. Her teeth were rotten."

"Now you are a landowner," Zak said.

"Ha. We had to fight for this land and we stole sheep from the Navajo, who stole their sheep from someone else. There is no justice in the world."

They talked of the dead sheepherder lying somewhere out there in a field of grass. Gregorio spoke of irrigating their crops of millet and corn, the grasses and the beans, the tomatoes and yams, the hot chilis and garbanzo beans. All while the dead man and woman decayed and blowflies laid their eggs in their flesh and the votive candles flickered and released scents that could not hide the aroma of the dead.

Zak listened and did not talk much.

Before they both retired, he asked Gregorio just one question.

"This Narbona," he said, "how many years did he have, would you say?"

"He was young. He had no more than twenty-two or twenty-three years. All of the Navajos were young men, very strong. The gringos—the Americans—they had more years, maybe thirty or more."

Zak did not take the term "gringo" as an insult. He knew the origin of the word from tales told around the campfire. In the early days of Mexican contact with Americans, the Mexicans heard them singing "Green Grow the Lilacs." They heard "green grow" as "gringo," and the word became a handy nickname for the white men.

Zak thought of that on this early morn when the moon was high and full and the Milky Way stretched its glittering band across the heavens and Venus commanded a corner of the sky above the mountains, bright as a diamond. Young men with dead men's names. Not old men in their fifties or sixties, but young men in their twenties.

In the east Zak saw a thin crease in the sky, a spreading cream that was the dawn. The black velvet sky paled above that rent, and the stars, the Milky Way—all began to evaporate, leaving only the Morning Star, Venus, shining brightly just above the horizon. Then that star, too, disappeared and the dawn rose in all its splendor, spraying light on small puffs of clouds, turning the sky a pale robin's-egg blue.

There was a stirring in the house, and Zak heard the patter of sandals on hard-packed earth, the rattle of a wood stove, the clank of a coffee pot, the slosh of water from a bucket. His stomach roiled with hunger and a low growl indicated juices flowing in an empty cavity.

Moments later he turned to see Gregorio step through the door, disheveled from sleep, his clothes rumpled, his gray hair askew.

"Good morning, Zak," he said. "Did you sleep well?"

"Good morning, Gregorio. I slept like a baby with the itch."

Gregorio laughed, then coughed up night phlegm, hawking the gob onto the ground.

"You make the joke, Zak."

"I slept."

"With one eye open, eh?"

"Sometimes two. Like an owl."

Gregorio laughed again, not so hearty this time, as he stepped alongside Zak.

"The water, it boils. Soon we will drink the coffee to clear our minds, then take a little breakfast, eh?"

"We have some digging to do. Do you know where you want to bury your relatives?"

"Yes. On a little hill where there is ocotillo and paloverde. And we must find Juanito Salazar and lay him to rest as well." He paused for a moment, then said: "And the dogs. They must be buried with dignity."

"For sure," Zak said, the Spanish falling easily from his tongue.

Gregorio had a little flatbed cart in the barn, with handles on both ends. After breakfast the two men went to the pasture and found two dogs, small black-and-white border collies, and loaded their carcasses on the cart. They found the body of Salazar next to one of the irrigation ditches. They laid out the bodies next to a little hill, then went back to the house to get the other bodies. Gregorio had wrapped them in sheets, and he took another sheet with him for Salazar. He also took a bucket of water, a cloth, and soap. At the barn they loaded two shovels on the cart, one on either end.

Gregorio washed Salazar's face and around the bullet wound in his chest while Zak began to dig the graves. He could hear Gregorio chanting soft prayers over the three corpses and the two dogs.

Gregorio dug the two graves for his brother and sister-in-law, dug through grass to rock, and for a long while the only sound was the ring of the shovels on stone. The sun rose and shrank the shadows, spread across the green fields and glinted off the river. Quail piped and doves whistled past them, their wings flashing teal as they flew downriver, and geese honked as they fed on the banks.

When they finished burying the two dogs and the three people, both men were soaked with sweat. They leaned on their shovels and looked at the mounds.

"I will make crosses," Gregorio said, and there were tears in his eyes. "I will remember them each day of my life."

Zak said nothing. He could feel the man's grief. It lay like a heavy weight between them as the old man wept silently.

Finally, Gregorio knelt on one knee and crossed himself. He said the prayers in a halting voice choked with emotion. They were simple prayers, composed on the spot, prayers that seemed to come from somewhere deep in Gregorio's heart and mind. Zak bowed his head and breathed the air that drifted down from the high frozen peaks of the Sangre de Cristo range, which loomed over the hills in majestic splendor.

Later, when Zak was saddling Nox, Gregorio came up to him.

"What will you do about your sheep, Gregorio?"

"First I will ride to Santa Fe and tell the soldiers about Narbona and what happened here."

"There is no need. I will tell the soldiers."

"I must find men to help me tend the sheep. I must try and buy two more dogs."

"Will that be an easy thing to do?"

"I do not know. I must do these things. And I must tell the soldiers, as Narbona ordered me to do."

"I will tell the soldiers."

"You are going to Santa Fe?"

"Not today. I am going to track Narbona and find out where he goes."

"Ah, that will be very dangerous, Zak. You are one man. They are many."

"This I must do."

"Who are you?" Gregorio asked. "I know what you are called, but who are you? Why do you come here?"

Zak did not want to tell him much, but the man deserved some kind of answer.

"You say, Gregorio, that there is no justice in the world. I am a man who does not believe that. I bring justice with me for such men as Narbona. For bad men."

"Who pays you to do this?"

Zak pulled the single cinch tight through the D ring, wrapped the leather into a loop, and ran the end through the loop and pulled it tight. Nox swelled his belly and Zak bumped him with the back of his hand where he had swelled. The air went out and Zak tightened the cinch even more, until the saddle was secure on the horse's back.

"The United States pays me," Zak said.

"Ah, you are a soldier?"

"I was a soldier. Now I ride alone."

Gregorio took a step backward and cocked his head as he looked Zak up and down. "You have the bearing of a soldier," he said, "but you have the look of a hunter. You ride alone, and I have heard of such a man. They call him *jinete de sombra*. Is this you, on your black horse, wearing the black clothing? Are you the one they call Shadow Rider?"

"I am a friend," Zak said, "who hopes that he will see you again, Gregorio. I share the grief you carry in your heart and I will take the memory of your tragedy with me. I will carry justice with me. Justice will be in the bullets that I put in my rifle and pistol and in my bare hands. That is all that you need to know."

Zak climbed into the saddle as Gregorio stared at him with a look of wonder on his face.

"Go with God," Gregorio breathed. "Beware of Narbona. There is a red flower in the blade of his knife."

"I know," Zak said. He had heard the comment before, from some poet born in Mexico. The knife flower. He knew what it meant. Blood sprouted from the blade of a knife into a crimson blossom. It was a hideous thought, but it was also very beautiful.

"Have care where you ride, Zak," Gregorio said. "You do not have fear?"

Zak touched a finger to the brim of his hat and started to ride out of the barn.

"I am the fear of Narbona," Zak said. "I am the fear that comes in the deep of night and walks in his dreams. I am the fear that comes when a man is standing before a firing squad with a dozen rifles aimed at his heart. I do not fear. I *am* fear."

Zak rode out, down through the green pasture and onto the track of the men who had spilled the blood of innocents and stolen that which could not ever be given back: life. There was steel in his jaw and a fierce glint in his eye.

He turned and waved to Gregorio, who stood in front of the house in all his sadness and grief, a man who knew that there truly was no justice in the world.

And even if there was, it could not bring the dead back to life.

4

Zak heard the pitiful bleating not long after he entered a small canyon where the tracks had led him. Narbona had driven off a dozen sheep after killing the Delacruz husband and wife. That much, the tracks had shown. Now they told another story. Before entering the canyon, the shod horses veered off to the south. The separation, evidently, had been prearranged. None of the horses had stopped. It was a case of the white men veering off while the Navajos continued on into the foothills. The sheep went with the Indians. The white men rode off together. Zak followed the Navajo and sheep tracks.

Not many sheep for a raider, Zak thought.

Now, in late afternoon, he heard sheep where no sheep should be.

He rounded a bend and saw them. The sheep were all bunched together, bleating like lost souls. They started to run when they saw Zak and Nox, all of them moving at once. They ran only a short distance, still bunched up, and stood there, all of them staring at him and pleading to be rescued.

It was plain to Zak that the raiding party had stopped there in that small bowl in the canyon. He took his time deciphering the maze of tracks—horse and sheep, white men and Indians. Yes, Narbona had felt safe in that place, but he had posted lookouts or guards at the east entrance and, from the dried blood pools and the pair of fleecy hides, had butchered two sheep.

He found a crumpled-up wad of paper and thin cardboard that told Zak what brand of store-boughts at least one of the white men smoked. He picked it up, smoothed it out, and read the label: PIEDMONT. He discarded the empty pack and climbed back on his horse. He estimated that the raiding party had spent less than an hour there. He was somewhat surprised that Narbona had left ten sheep alive. Did he expect someone to find them and retrieve them? Did he want to leave such a bold trail, at least to that point?

The more he studied the behavior of Narbona and the others in his party, the more puzzled Zak became.

He took one last look at the frightened sheep and vowed to drive them out of the canyon on his return trip. They would suffer a horrible death by starvation if he did not do this. The sheep were lost and could not be expected to find their way back to the ranch from whence they had come.

He rode on, more slowly than before, scanning the rimrock, studying the tracks. Narbona seemed in no hurry, but Zak was convinced that the man had a destination. The canyon petered out, opening up onto a broad sandy wash, and he found himself on a small ridge in a maze of ridges, a foothill region that was rugged and exposed. A dangerous place if men were stationed on the high reaches watching Narbona's back trail.

The small highway of tracks exploded from single file to a burst of individual hoofprints that spread out, fanlike, in a dozen directions. Once away from the sandy wash, the individual tracks vanished on the myriad of small ridges that fanned out from that place. Not one man or a dozen could follow such a dispersion of horses without ending up lost, crazy, or shot dead. Narbona knew that country, Zak decided, and so did the men who rode with him.

For all practical purposes, the entire band of thieves and assassins had vanished into thin air.

Zak turned his horse, ventured back into the small canyon, back to where the sheep were bunched together in fear of the unknown. As he rode, he wondered about the soldiers, who, back in the 1840s, had ventured into the Jemez looking for Navajos to round up and put on reservations. They had hauled mountain howitzers and field guns over treacherous terrain, and the Navajos had melted into the mountains and become like smoke, most never to be found.

He drove the sheep back out onto the plain, herding them slowly, cutting back and forth to guide them, keep them from scattering in all directions. Nox became a sheepdog, and the horse didn't like it. Neither did the sheep.

He left them as close to Gregorio's ranch as he could and then doubled back to pick up the tracks of the two white men, known to him only as Ralph and Pete. Their tracks were easy to follow, even though they were now over twenty hours old. They went south, then turned east. Eventually, the two men had reached a well-traveled road that paralleled the Rio Grande. Cart tracks, mules, burros, and horses made it difficult to sort out the hoof marks of the two men. Zak almost lost them in a maze of deer tracks and other animal tracks where Pete and Ralph had left the road and headed for the river across rocky and uneven ground.

The tracks led to a ford in a wide part of the river. The water was shallow in places, but Nox slipped into deep water at one point and had to swim back to a place where his hooves could touch the hard bottom. He climbed out, dripping wet, and shook himself before they could proceed further. It took Zak a few minutes to find the tracks of the two white men again.

Zak lost the tracks of the two men again when they joined a road that was seeing heavy traffic. Men riding on carts pulled by burros, boys on mules and men on horseback, people on foot, all seemed to be going in one direction: toward Santa Fe. A few miles from the city Zak stopped to rest Nox and study the maze of tracks. He could not find those made by the men he had been following. He was well off the road, gazing at the Sangre de Cristos, when he saw a dust cloud to the north. The sun was falling away in the western sky by then, the almost cloudless sky painted a vivid cobalt blue. Few people passed by, but the cloud of dust drew closer and closer. Then the dust lessened and he was about to resume riding toward Santa Fe when he saw the dark horses emerge from the dust. They stopped and he saw a sharp glint of sunlight. It looked as if someone had brought a telescope up and was ranging with it, swinging it slowly back and forth to scan the landscape.

A few moments later, as he rode slowly toward the advancing men on horseback, Zak saw the blue uniforms, the yellow stripes on trouser legs, the shine of boots and brass. No guidon, he noticed. But cavalry troopers, four or five men riding, single file, straight toward him.

As they drew closer Zak saw that the horses were shiny with sweat and the uniforms caked with dust. The road suddenly emptied of all traffic. Zak kept on his course, but an uneasy feeling began to grow in him. Where had all the people gone? Why had the horses been at a gallop and then suddenly taken to a walk?

The horses broke into a gallop again. Zak felt his throat go dry. His mouth tasted of copper as the ripping hooves stirred up dust that grew like clouds and took on the colors of the land, tinted cinnamon and rust, lavender and a fine gold turned to mist. He turned Nox onto a side road to get out of the way, and heard a shout.

"You there. Halt. You on the black horse."

He reined in Nox and turned to face the oncoming riders.

There were only four of them, a second lieutenant, a sergeant, and two corporals.

They reined up within ten yards of where Zak was sitting on his horse, the sun beaming on his sun-browned face and glistening on Nox's hide like polished ebony.

As soon as they halted, the enlisted men drew Spencer carbines from their rifle scabbards and aimed them at Zak. The lieutenant drew his pistol.

Then the men fanned out so that they were all aiming weapons at him from various directions.

Zak did not move.

"Hands in the air," the lieutenant said.

"Why?"

"You heard me. Put up those hands or we'll shoot you right out of the saddle."

There was no mistaking the man's belligerence. He was young, with that fresh-faced look of a boy who has suddenly grown into manhood but does not have to shave every day. The sergeant was older, perhaps thirty or so, and the corporals both looked like schoolboys.

"All right," Zak said, and slowly raised both hands. He turned the palms outward to show that he had no weapon in either hand.

"Corporal Mead," the lieutenant said, "you and Corporal Davis relieve that man of his weapons."

"Yes, sir," the two young corporals said. They spurred their horses and rode toward Zak, their rifles leveled at him.

"I hope those rifles are on safety," Zak said when the troopers halted on either side of him.

"Shut up," the lieutenant ordered.

The corporals did as they were ordered. One took Zak's rifle; the other lifted his pistol from its holster. They turned their horses and rode back, Zak's weapons in their awkward hands.

The lieutenant and the sergeant rode up close.

"State your name and your business, mister," the lieutenant said.

"What's this all about, Lieutenant?"

"I'll ask the questions here."

"May I lower my hands?" Zak said.

"Easy. Real easy, mister."

Zak lowered his hands, folded them over his saddle horn. He could smell the sweat-fear on the lieutenant's body. He saw the uncertainty in his eyes, the nervousness rippling through the meat of his legs and the tendons in his arms, the slight tremor in the hand that held the pistol. This was no battle-hardened cavalryman, but a man more at home on an army post than out in the field.

"The name's Zak Cody."

"What's your business?"

"I'm not at liberty to say."

"What's that mean?" snapped the lieutenant.

"It means I cannot tell you my business, Lieutenant. It's my business, and no other's."

"I don't like your answer."

"Take it or leave it," Zak said.

"Sergeant, I want this man's hands cuffed. He'll be in irons by nightfall."

The sergeant didn't move, but continued to stare at Zak with a curious intensity.

"Sergeant Bullard," the lieutenant barked.

"Sir, beggin' your pardon, sir, but I heard that name Cody before. And I heard the name Zak Cody more'n once."

"What do you mean, Bullard?"

"I mean, I think this man's army. In some way."

Bullard spoke in a halting, awkward meter, as if he were trying to figure out something he didn't quite understand.

"Army?" The lieutenant's face bore a puzzled look.

"Kind of. Yes, sir."

"Cody, do you know what the sergeant's talking about?"

"Not exactly," Zak said.

"Are you in the army, mister? What are you, a deserter?"

"No, I'm not a deserter. And, strictly speaking, I'm not in the U.S. Army anymore."

"This is a lot of double-talk as far as I'm concerned." The lieutenant's eyes sparked with anger. "Mister, I want straight answers and I want them now."

"Sir, I believe this man Cody once worked for General Crook. I think he still does, but not so's he can talk about it. Just what I heard from others."

"Barracks gossip, Sergeant."

"No, sir. From other officers, some who served with Crook and fought with him. It's some kind of secret. Ain't nobody supposed to know about Zak Cody. I think he still carries a commission."

"Is that so, Cody?" The lieutenant's tone had changed ever so slightly.

"Is what so?" Zak said.

"That you are a commissioned officer in the U.S. Army? Under secret orders?"

Zak smiled.

"Well, now, if this was so, Lieutenant, and I told you, it wouldn't be a secret anymore, would it?"

"Give me some kind of answer or I'll be forced to clap you in handcuffs."

"Straight or crooked?" Zak asked.

"What?"

"The answer you want, Lieutenant."

"I want proof of who you are and if you have rank I want to know what it is."

Zak skewered the lieutenant with a hard look. The corporals looked like a couple of kids about to see a school whipping but not sure who was going to get it. Sergeant Bullard's jaw tightened and he lowered the barrel of his rifle. It was almost like a salute, or a sign of surrender. He put a hand to his throat and stroked the stubble underneath. He looked as if he wanted to be anyplace other than where he was now.

The lieutenant swallowed and his face began to pale. He drew in a breath and let it out again through his nostrils. He looked as if he was going to be sick.

"You come close, Lieutenant," Zak said. "Just you, and put that pistol back in your holster. Ride real close and ride real slow."

There was no mistaking the authority in Zak's voice.

It carried all the weight and shine of a cavalry sword, and every uniformed man there knew it. For a long moment it seemed as if all four soldiers were in shock, frozen in place on a deserted plain, immobile as statues in a Wild West museum.

5

The lieutenant hesitated, but only for a second or two.

Then he holstered his pistol, closed the flap on his holster. He ticked blunt spurs into his horse's flanks and moved up close to Zak, a querulous look on his face.

"And I'll have your name, Lieutenant," Zak said.

"I'm Second Lieutenant Harvey Walsh," he rasped.

"Lean close to me so I can whisper in your ear, Walsh," Zak said.

Walsh did as he was told, a sheepish look on his face, as if it were covered in boiled oatmeal.

Zak put his mouth close to Walsh's ear.

"I carry the rank of colonel," Zak said. "I'm under secret orders from President Grant and General Crook. That's all you need to know right now, Walsh. And keep this information to yourself."

"Yes, sir," Walsh breathed. "I mean, yes, Colonel."

"Not a word, now."

"No, sir."

Zak sat up straight in his saddle.

"Now," he said, in his normal speaking voice,

"I'll have my rifle and pistol returned to me, Lieutenant Walsh."

"Sergeant Bullard, see to it that Co—Mr. Cody's rifle and pistol are returned to him. Posthaste."

"Yes, sir," Bullard said and turned to the corporals. Both rode forward. One handed the rifle to Zak, the other his pistol. Zak slid the Winchester back in its boot and holstered his pistol.

"Now, Mr. Walsh," Zak said, "tell me why you stopped me and used force."

Walsh reached in his shirt pocket and pulled out a small metal mirror. The mirror had a cross cut into it. He held it up until it caught the sun's rays, flashed a light toward the foothills. He moved the mirror so that its beams struck a high point on one of the hills. A moment later there was a series of answering flashes.

"We have a detail on the other side of the river," Walsh said. "They watched you driving some sheep and grew suspicious. They watched you cross the river and head this way. I rode to intercept you."

"Fair enough," Zak said. "Tell those troops that all is well."

Walsh worked the mirror and flashed the troops on the hill. They flashed back and Walsh slid the mirror back in his pocket.

"What were you doing with those sheep?" Walsh asked.

"A long story. Call me Zak. I'll call you Harvey."

"Yes, sir."

"And no 'sirs.' "

"No, sir." Walsh gulped air down his throat. "I mean . . ."

"I know what you mean, Harvey. Now, who's over there in the hills, the signaler?"

"Captain Jeffrey Vickers. We've been splitting up patrols, trying to cover both sides of the Rio Grande."

"What's the assignment?"

"Reports of theft. Cattle, sheep, and the like. People come into the Presidio to complain and we're trying to find out who's stealing all that stock."

"And who do you think is stealing the stock, Harvey?"

"It doesn't make much sense. The farmers and ranchers are saying it's Navajos. The Mexicans are superstitious. They report they're being raided by a ghost warrior. Captain Vickers was assigned to track down the rustlers and put those rumors to rest."

"Ghost warrior?" Zak said. He realized that the sun would soon set and Vickers would no longer be able to use the signaling mirror. But Harvey could still get a message off. He held up his hand and measured the distance between the sun and the tops of the Sangre de Cristos. Two fingers' distance. That meant the sun would disappear in about a half an hour. Fifteen minutes to a finger.

"Yes, that's right."

"Harvey, I want you to flash Captain Vickers and tell him to stay put. Tell him we'll join him shortly after nightfall."

"Sir, I mean, Zak, I can't do that. I have orders . . ."

"I'm countermanding those orders. It's very important that I talk to Vickers before he makes another move."

"Well, I guess. Since you outrank me. It's highly irregular, though."

"All right, Harvey," Zak said. "Flash Vickers to hold his position."

Walsh took out his signaling mirror and began to flash the far hills. Zak read the message while he looked at the sergeant and the other two men. The two corporals couldn't have been more than eighteen years old, and they looked as green as any raw recruit.

When Walsh finished sending the message, they both stared at the hills. Walsh reached into his saddlebag and pulled out his telescope. He aimed it where he thought Vickers was encamped. Zak saw some flashes, but they were so quick and small he couldn't read them with accuracy.

"Did you get his reply?" Zak asked.

"Yes. He just said he was breaking camp."

"Is that all?"

"That's all he said."

Zak saw no more flashes from the Vickers camp. He said nothing for several seconds as he regarded the two enlisted men wearing corporal chevrons. Bullard was reaching into his pocket for something. A moment later he pulled out a package of store-bought cigarettes. He took one out and struck a match, lit it. Then he put the package back in his pocket.

"Harvey," Zak said, "I want to send a message to your commanding officer. He at the Presidio?"

"Yes, he is. Lieutenant Colonel Jeremiah Loomis."

"Got paper and pencil?"

"Of course. I keep field notes, Zak. I was going to turn them in to Colonel Loomis tonight."

Zak watched the sun sinking toward the horizon. The ermine peaks of the Sangre de Cristos gleamed with a pristine brilliance, as if someone had drenched the granite with fresh whitewash. His heart was sinking with the sun. Why was Vickers breaking camp? Was he returning to Santa Fe? Not likely. He had seen something or suspected something and was going on the march. And it was late in the day to mount an expedition in that rugged country.

Walsh produced his notebook and a pencil. He opened the book to a blank sheet and held the pencil, hovering, just above the page.

"Take this down," Zak said. "Crossing Rio Grande to join forces with Captain Vickers. Do not send more troops to investigate Navajo rustlers until further notice."

"Is that the entire message? Colonel Loomis will throw a fit."

"Sign your name per Colonel Zak Cody, then date it and note the time of day. Send both corporals to the Presidio with that message, and make sure they deliver it to Loomis in person."

Walsh signed the document, tore it out of the book, folded it, and beckoned to the two corporals. "Mead and Davis, take this message to the Presidio of Santa Fe. Deliver it to Colonel Loomis posthaste."

"Then, stay there," Zak added.

"Yes."

"Both of us?" Mead asked.

"Both of you. Quick." Walsh handed the folded note to Mead. Both men saluted. Mead put the message in his pocket and both men rode off toward Santa Fe.

"You still going back to the hills, Zak?" Walsh asked. "There's only three of us and that's dangerous country over there."

"Three will be enough," Zak said. Then he added, "I hope."

"May I ask what your intentions are?" Walsh said.

"I'm going to try and head off Captain Vickers and his men before they ride right into a trap," Zak said.

"What trap?"

The sound of the galloping horses faded away in the evening air. Spools of dust fanned out and turned to a fine scrim that looked like a golden mist in the sunlight.

Zak didn't answer right away. He rode over to Sergeant Bullard and took the cigarette out of his hand, then gave it back to him.

"Piedmont?" Zak said.

"Yes, sir. Fine smokes. Want one?"

"No. Where do you buy those? On the post?"

Bullard laughed.

"No, sir. I get those at Biederman's Saloon and General Store. Only place in Santa Fe you can buy 'em."

"You'll have to take me there, one of these days," Zak said.

"Be glad to, sir."

"No more 'sirs,' Sergeant. Just call me Zak. As far as you're concerned, unless I give you a military order, I'm a civilian."

"Yes, sir. I mean . . ."

"Good enough," Zak said, then turned to Walsh. "What was your question, Harvey?"

"You mentioned a trap. What trap?"

"I don't know," Zak said. "How are you and Bullard fixed for provisions?"

"We're just about out of hardtack and jerky. We were heading back to the Presidio when we caught up with you."

"We might have to live off the land for a few days. You up to it?"

"I don't know. You mean rabbits and squirrels?"

"Maybe lizards and rattlesnakes."

Walsh's face drained of color and he swallowed another gulp of New Mexican air.

Bullard suppressed a chuckle.

"Let's get to it," Zak said, turning his horse. The two soldiers flanked him and they rode back toward the river and the ford where Zak had crossed.

Zak held the flat of his hand up to the western horizon again. One finger.

Fifteen minutes of daylight left.

But he knew the trail, and the moon would be almost full. He'd find Vickers if he could, if not that night, then early in the morning.

He hoped he wouldn't be too late.

⚡ **6** ⚡

The setting sun gilded the far clouds to a burnished sheen, set the skies aglow with soft fire, painted the river a metallic array of colors that looked like hammered silver, gold, and magenta. Blue-winged teal flew upriver on whistling wings and turned to shadow in the gathering dusk. By the time Zak and the two troopers reached the river, the clouds were ashes in the sky and frogs bellowed and grunted along the banks like grumpy old men standing in a grub line.

Zak led the way, traversing the ford by dead reckoning as the sky turned dark as pitch and Venus rose high and shining in the paling afterglow of sunset. The stars emerged on a black velvet tapestry while the ground ahead of them turned into a tar pit with no definition, and all landmarks receded into mysteries, of strange shapes carved out of ebony or black coal.

The going was slow—treacherous—over rough ground. Zak deliberately kept Nox to a slow walk and the horse was not averse to this, for his eyesight was no better than the humans' in such a black morass. Zak used the stars to guide him, in particular the pole star of the Big Dipper, but he also was steering Nox by dead reckoning. He had fixed on a point where he had abandoned the ten sheep while it was still light and knew they would not drift far. He listened for the first calls of coyotes or wolves, because he knew these predators would be heading for the same destination. He kept on, waiting for the first complaint from Lieutenant Walsh, which he knew would come.

"Begging your pardon, Zak," Walsh said, after an hour of riding blind under Zak's leadership, "but how do you expect to locate Captain Vickers in the dark? I can't make out any trails or roads, nor do I have any idea where we are."

"My guess is," Zak said, "that Captain Vickers will encounter the same difficulty. I believe he left his observation post to find some stray sheep I left up there. He will probably want to check ear brands and find out which ranch they were stolen from. I gather he has a brand book with him."

"He does," Walsh said. "He has a little book with some cow and sheep brands, who they're registered to, and a map of ranches and farms all up and down the Rio Grande. But, how in hell is he going to find anything out here? The mountains make it so black you can't find your face with both hands."

"Right. So, I have another guess that I hope pans out."

"And what is that, pray tell?"

"Captain Vickers, whether he finds the sheep or not, will make another camp, somewhere closer to where we are now."

"Yes?"

"He will most likely build a fire and post pickets. He'll boil some coffee, maybe make some bannock or fry some meat for supper."

"What makes you think that?" Walsh asked.

"When a man is not used to the wilderness, he builds a fire at night. There will be wolves and coyotes slinking around, especially if he camps near those sheep."

"Are you saying Captain Vickers is afraid of the dark?"

"Maybe not afraid of the dark, Harvey, but maybe a little uncomfortable in it. He's probably civilized and is used to oil lamps and four walls. Out here, he has only darkness and the stars."

Walsh was silent for a few minutes. The only sounds were the ring of iron horseshoes on stone and the scuff of hooves on gravelly soil.

Zak heard a rustling sound from Bullard's direction.

"Don't light a cigarette, Sergeant," Zak said.

"No? Why not, sir? I mean Zak."

"You might attract a Navajo brave, Bullard."

"Out here? Hell, what are they, owls?"

"This is Navajo country, or was, and they can grow out of the ground," Zak said.

"Huh?"

"A band of them attacked a sheep rancher yesterday. Killed a herder, and another man and his wife. Couple of sheepdogs, too."

"You think they're still out here?" Walsh asked.

"It might be good for you to think that they're all around us."

"You're trying to scare us, Zak," Walsh said. "Aren't you?"

"Are you scared, Harvey?"

The lieutenant did not answer right away. As if he was mulling the question over in his mind.

"I'm somewhat apprehensive," Walsh said.

"Good. Stay that way. You'll live longer, maybe."

"Christ," Bullard cursed, and put away the pack of cigarettes.

An hour later the moon began to rise through a dove-gray cloudbank. Its feeble light cast a pewter haze over the broken land, making the going even more difficult. Rocks and plants twisted into grotesque shapes, seemed to shift position from one glance to another, as if the country were playing tricks on any who passed over it. Zak, who was used to such distortions at night, did not look directly at any minor landmarks, but gazed above or below them, and thus was able to guide the two men onward, where others might have stumbled and become discouraged.

They traversed the plain and rode onto gradually rising land. The moon drifted ever higher and shed the cloud bank, leaving behind a clump of long dark clouds that resembled ashen loaves of bread.

On the edge of the foothills, perhaps a mile or so away, Zak saw a flickering orange flame. It was barely visible, as if there was a fire in a pit or a depression. He reined up Nox and turned to Walsh, putting a finger to his lips to indicate silence. Zak pointed up the slope until Walsh nodded. Bullard nodded, too.

Zak leaned close to Walsh.

"If there are pickets, is there a password?"

"Not that I know of," Walsh said.

"Then we must be careful. If that's Vickers up there, we don't want his men shooting at us."

"Right."

"Just follow me. Real slow and real quiet."

Both the lieutenant and the sergeant nodded.

Zak did not ride straight to where the campfire was burning. Instead, he angled off to the left in order to make a wide circle and come up above the camp. It would take extra time, but if Vickers was camped there, he would have guards posted and they might be trigger happy.

The moon sailed free of the clouds and cast a hazy light over the land. The shapes of rocks and cactus and ocotillo did not shift so much. The landscape was in sharp relief, in fact, glazed with a wash of light. In the distance, a coyote yapped, then others answered with high-pitched ribbons of melodic howls that ascended the scale. They were far away, up one of the canyons, but Zak knew they had scented or spotted game.

They reached a point above the campfire and started riding toward it. Zak motioned for Walsh and Bullard to spread out and ride a little behind him. He forced Nox into a very slow walk, let the horse pick its way over the noisy rocks and find soft sand and gravel where he could step without clanking his iron horseshoes on hard stone.

Then Zak held up his hand, signaling the soldiers to stop. They both reined up and Zak stared down at a bare spot on the ground right next to his horse. He couldn't be sure, but he thought he saw a fresh moccasin track. He closed his eyes and opened them again. The track was still there, oddly distinct in the moonlight. He felt the hairs on the back of his neck stiffen and a slight shiver run up his spine.

Something was not right. If that was a fresh track, then who had built the fire: friend or foe?

He turned to Walsh and Bullard and signaled for them to stay put. He dismounted, handed Nox's reins to Walsh. Again, he held a finger to his lips.

Zak began to walk toward the firelight, stepping carefully, letting his forward foot settle on bare ground before putting his weight on it. He crept, hunched over, for some twenty yards, then froze. He saw a dark shape on the ground. A shape that was not a rock or a bush. Again, the hairs on the back of his neck prickled.

Now Zak heard voices, low-pitched, coming from the area of the campfire. He listened for several seconds and determined that he was listening to the English tongue. He let out a breath and continued toward the hulking shape. It took him only a moment to see what it was—the body of a soldier. The soldier wasn't asleep. He was dead.

Zak felt for the pulse in the man's neck. There was none. He put a hand on his back and it came away sticky with blood. He turned the soldier over and saw the deep slash in his throat. He ran his hands all over the body. There was no pistol, no ammunition case. No rifle. Whoever had killed the soldier had stripped him clean of weapons and ammunition. Even his campaign hat was missing, along with his yellow scarf.

Zak stood up.

He walked toward the fire, still in a crouch. When he got close enough to hear the conversations, he stood up. He counted four men, all soldiers, sitting around the fire, smoking and talking.

"Hello, the campfire," Zak called, loud enough for all the soldiers there to hear him.

The soldiers stiffened and moved. One grabbed up a rifle, another drew his pistol. They all stared into the darkness, their eyes blinded by the bright firelight.

"Who—Who goes there?" called the man with the rifle.

"Lieutenant Walsh and Sergeant Bullard," Zak said.

"Show yourselves."

Zak turned and whistled, beckoned to Walsh and Bullard to ride to him.

"We're coming," Zak said. "Just hold on."

"I don't recognize that voice," one of the men said.

"Me, neither," said another.

"Mister, you better walk up here, where's we can see you," the man with the rifle said.

"Just keep your pants on," Zak said. "Hear the horses? That's Walsh and Bullard."

"I hear 'em," said one.

Zak didn't see any officer in the group of men. They were all plainly visible. Easy targets. The fire had been built next to a large, flat rock that jutted from the ground. The rock reflected the heat onto a sizeable area, where bedrolls lay spread out for the night.

Walsh and Bullard rode up. Zak took Nox's reins from Walsh and signaled for him and Bullard to ride up to the camp. He followed, leading Nox, walking with a long stride until he was on the edge of the firelight.

"Lieutenant. What you doin' here this time of night?" a corporal asked.

"Where's Captain Vickers?" Walsh asked.

"Why, he and Sarge drove some sheep up the ways to a ranch. He found the brand. Wanted to question the owner. He said he'd be back soon's he delivered them sheep."

Zak stood there, just outside the edge of the firelight. "Corporal, how many men did you have on picket?"

The corporal turned toward him, shading his eyes to block out the light. "I can't see you, mister. Who you be?"

"Never mind that," Zak said. "Answer my question."

"Why, Private Kelso's over on our left flank and y'all should have seen Private Deming over yonder where y'all come from."

"Deming's dead," Zak said. "One of you better check on Kelso."

"Dead?" the corporal said.

"That's right. His throat's cut and he got a knife in his back. He was stripped clean of his rifle, pistol, and cartridges. If he carried a knife, that's gone, too."

"Shit," the corporal, named Fender, said. "Ol' Willie's dead?"

"Dead as you're going to be, Corporal," Zak said, "unless you put out that fire."

Corporal Fender looked up at Walsh. "Sir?" he said.

"Do what he says, Fender," Walsh said. "Jacobs, you check on Kelso. On the double."

A private picked up his rifle and ran off into the darkness. Fender and another man, Private Lewis Carlisle, started kicking dirt on the fire. The fire went out and the darkness surged over the camp, drowning all the men in shadow.

Zak walked up behind the flat rock and tied Nox to a bush. The other horses were further away, hobbled some fifty yards from the camp.

They all heard a curse coming from Private Leo Jacobs.

"Private Kelso's dead," he called, in a disembodied voice that didn't seem real to the men assembled there.

The silence welled up around them all as the last of the fire flickered out, leaving only the smell of wood smoke and death in the air.

Private Jacobs stumbled back into camp, out of breath.

"His throat was cut plumb to his backbone," he blurted out. "Poor Kelso. He never had a chance. Stabbed in the back, too."

"They take his weapons?" Zak asked.

"Yes, sir, they sure did. Even his kerchief was gone."

"Men, I suggest you all pick up your rifles, cock them, and just start listening," Zak said. "Lieutenant, you and Sergeant Bullard put your horses where mine is, but don't unsaddle them."

"What're we lookin' for?" Jacobs asked.

"Maybe nothing," Zak said. "Or maybe an Indian you'll never see."

"Huh?" Jacobs said.

"He means," Bullard said, "that they's Navajos skulkin' about and they might sneak up on you like they did Deming and Kelso."

"Shit," Jacobs said, and they could all detect the fear in his voice.

The soldiers all sat down in a semicircle. Zak stayed at the center, his back to all the men. He had a commanding view of the terrain below the camp as well as to both north and south. Under the glint of the moon, the Rio Grande was a silvery metal band that undulated in and out of shadow. He wanted to be the one to spot Captain Vickers when he and his sergeant returned. Since the two were on horseback, he knew they would come back sometime during the night.

"Did Captain Vickers know who owned those sheep?" Zak asked Corporal Fender.

"He read the markings in their ears: a *D* and a cross. He looked up the brand and then found the ranch on his map."

"Vickers have a compass with him?" Zak asked the corporal.

"Yes, sir, he sure did. He marked where we was on his map and said he'd be back sometime later."

"He tell you how far you were from that sheep ranch?"

"No, sir, he didn't."

It was quiet for a while, and then Zak heard the corporal whisper to Walsh.

"Who is that man, sir? He ain't army."

Zak could not hear Walsh's answer, but it seemed to satisfy Fender, because he shut up after that.

One of the privates spoke up after they all had been standing watch for more than an hour.

"If they's Injuns out there, how come they don't try and steal our horses?"

"That's a good question," Walsh said. "You got an answer, Zak?"

"I think those Navajos are trying to goad the army into going after them," Zak said.

"That doesn't make sense," Walsh said.

"No, it doesn't, does it?" Zak said.

He had been thinking about just that very question for a long while. Why did the Navajos kill those two soldiers and none of the others? Narbona had enough men to shoot every one of them while they sat by the fire. The soldiers were easy targets. Instead, he or his braves had sneaked up on the two guards, cut their throats, and taken their weapons and ammunition. If he was just trying to get arms, he could have had four more rifles and as many pistols.

No, it didn't make sense, unless Narbona wanted to draw the army out, make soldiers take to the field and come after him. And, no doubt, the Navajo had a plan to wipe out an entire company. But why? What would he gain by such tactics? He'd bring more soldiers down on him, seasoned men who, like Kit Carson, would hunt them down and either kill or capture every one of them.

No, there had to be a deeper reason for Narbona's actions. And why were two white men involved? They might be the key to why Narbona was attacking ranchers yet not stealing much. They might be the go-betweens for someone else, someone who wanted the army either to look bad or to fail in its pursuit of Navajo raiders.

Each question Zak asked himself dredged up more questions.

And no answer to any of them.

It began to turn cold, and Zak could hear the men shivering, their teeth chattering. The horses whickered and pawed the ground with their front hooves. A pack of coyotes started singing; the direction of the chorus shifted and faded, then died out. Zak couldn't see his breath yet, but he knew he would before morning.

Another hour went by and the silence was broken only by men clearing their throats, moving their feet to induce circulation in their legs. Zak put his hands under his armpits to keep them warm. If he had to draw his pistol he didn't want to grab the butt with a bunch of chilled bananas.

The moon sailed high in the sky, an alabaster globe that shed its light over a land of desolation and emptiness, rocks and plants all looking like the huddled figures of Navajo warriors just waiting to pounce.

"Where in hell is Cap'n Vickers?" one of the soldiers said.

"Shut up," whispered Walsh.

"Hell, sir, they ain't nobody out here but us," Corporal Fender said.

"I told you to shut up, Corporal." Zak could hear the irritation in Walsh's voice. But there was frustration, too.

Then he heard the faintest far-off sound. A scrape, a muffled clank of a horseshoe against a rock.

"Sergeant Bullard," Zak said. "You can light a cigarette now. Don't shield the flame. Anybody else who wants a smoke can light up."

"Thank you, sir," Bullard replied. A moment later there was the scratch of a match head on a rock, and a small flame flared in the darkness.

A couple of the other men lit up.

"What's going on, Zak?" Walsh asked.

"I think Vickers is looking for his camp."

"Cap'n Vickers?" Mead said. "Where?"

"Just hold your horses, Corporal," Walsh said, as all the matches fluttered out.

The men shuffled around, each trying to locate Captain Vickers to the north. Even with the moonlight glaring down on them, none could see anything.

Zak heard the scuff of a hoof now and then, and he had a general idea where Vickers and his sergeant were. They were moving slowly. A few minutes later he heard muffled voices and saw the dim shapes of two horses.

"They must have found the dead trooper," Zak said.

"I see 'em," Private Carlisle said.

"Me, too," Jacobs said.

"We all see 'em, boys," Bullard said, and then the men stopped talking as they stared off in the distance.

"Light another match, Bullard," Zak said.

"Looks like they're loading up Kelso," Walsh said.

Several minutes later Captain Vickers rode up, followed by Sergeant Renaldo Dominguez.

"Go help Sergeant Dominguez, Mitch," Bullard said to Corporal Fender. "Leave your rifle here."

Jeff Vickers was a short, wiry man with a cavalry moustache, neatly trimmed sideburns, square shoulders, and a ramrod for a backbone. Spit and polish, all the way, Zak thought. He sat there as the captain dismounted, looked at all the men.

"Who're you?" he said to Zak.

"Captain," Walsh broke in, "that's Zak Cody."

"What the hell's a civilian doing up here? Corporal Davis, take my horse. And what are you doing here, Harv?"

"Didn't you get my last message, sir?" Walsh said.

"No, I sure as hell didn't. Now, somebody better answer my question about this civilian and tell me why we had to stumble up here in the dark. I told you, Mead, to keep that fire going. And who the hell killed Kelso?"

Zak stood up.

"You know, Captain," he said, "you're not going to learn much by asking so many questions all at once."

"Stand down, mister," Vickers said. "When I want some of your mouth, I'll ask for it. I'm in charge here and as far as I'm concerned, you're as out of place as a turd in a punchbowl."

"Now, hold on, Captain," Walsh said, stepping up close to Vickers. "Don't jump to any conclusions."

"Lieutenant, you're just on the edge of being insubordinate. I want some answers here, and I want 'em real quick."

Zak towered over Vickers as he took another step, which put him toe to toe with the captain.

"Captain, I think I can answer all your questions," Zak said. "And I have every right to be here, so back off."

"Why you . . ." Vickers drew a gauntlet from his belt and raised his hand as if to strike Zak. Walsh lashed out his arm and grabbed the captain's wrist.

"I wouldn't do that, sir, if I were you."

"Walsh, you're—" Zak snatched the glove from Vickers' hand and slapped the captain hard across the mouth with it. Vickers' eyes went wide and his head snapped back, more in surprise than from the blow.

Walsh gasped.

Sergeant Dominguez and Mitch Fender came up. The body of Private Kelso was draped over the saddle on the sergeant's horse.

"Lieutenant," Zak said, "tell the captain about General Crook and President Grant." There was urgency in his voice.

Zak tucked Vickers' gauntlet back in his belt as Walsh leaned close to the captain and whispered into his ear.

"Is this true, Cody?" Vickers said when Walsh was finished talking to him.

"Is what true, Vickers?"

"That you're in the—"

"Vickers, whatever Harvey told you about me, keep it to yourself."

"I want to know if it's true."

Zak blew air out through his nostrils. Everyone there, except Vickers, knew that Zak was running out of patience.

"You can assume what Harvey told you is true, Captain," Zak said. "Now, you take a little walk with me and I'll answer all your questions. Bullard, send someone to bring in Deming. The captain might as well know the worst, right off."

"I'll go get Paul," Jacobs said. "Lew, you can help me. I know right where he is." Carlisle and Jacobs set their rifles down on the ground and stole off into the darkness. Zak took Vickers by the arm and led him off away from the other men. Bullard helped Fender lift Kelso's body off the horse. They did it gently, and laid the dead soldier out a couple of feet from the flat rock.

"Are you in the army, or aren't you, Cody?" Vickers said when they were out of earshot of the others.

"Still asking questions, are you, Vickers?"

"I have a right to know. I'm in command here. This is an army operation."

"It's an operation, all right," Zak said. "And you're lying on the table with a scalpel about to rip your belly open."

"See here, Cody—"

"No, you see here, Vickers. If you say one more word about your rank and your authority, you'll wonder if I'm the rug."

"The rug?"

"The rug that's going to be pulled out from under you, dumping you on your pompous little ass."

"Sir, I . . ."

Zak didn't lift a hand. He stood there glaring at Vickers, blowing air out of his nostrils like a bull when it's about to charge and gore a man to death with both horns.

Zak let Vickers' anger subside. "Are you listening, Vickers?" Zak said. "Don't open your mouth. Just nod or shake your head. You're in church now, mister. And I'm the preacher."

Vickers nodded, but he couldn't help himself. He asked the question.

"Ch–Church?"

"Yes, church," Zak said. "My church. And I'm going to read you chapter and verse."

Vickers swallowed a hard lump of nothing in his throat and clamped his mouth shut. He looked, Zak thought, like a snapping turtle, complete with a face that was turning menopause green.

It is during those post-midnight hours of the nocturnal cycle that the earth cools and gives up its scents along with its heat. There was the smell of burnt cedar and piñon from the campfire, the cloying fragrance of man-sweat and blood, the sandy scent of scorched earth and another that was almost indefinable, the aroma of fear mingled with the passing spoor of Navajo who made no sound, like the skulking wolf or the padding cougar up on the rimrock.

"You West Point?" Zak asked Vickers, his voice pitched low but with a timbre that struck the eardrums and made a man listen with all his might.

"VMI."

"Virginia Military Institute. William T. Sherman. Cumpy."

"Yes, he was one of my instructors before the war," Vickers said.

"Good man," Zak said. "He knew how to stop a war in its tracks. That's what I'm hoping to do."

"Stop a war?"

"If I can."

"What war?"

"The war that's just over the horizon, a war that will bring back all the old hates, all the old enemies and soak this fair land with blood and bleach the bones of many a promising young man."

"You—You're the one that the Mexican sheep rancher talked about, aren't you?" There was an undertone of awe and sudden revelation in Vickers' voice. "You're the one who found those sheep that belonged to Delacruz."

"Did Gregorio tell you what happened to his brother and his sister-in-law, his dogs, and one of his herders?"

"He did," Vickers said. "He spoke in Spanish, which is a tongue I'm trying to master. He called you something like 'horseman of the shadow.' And now I'm remembering some stories I heard since I came out West. Stories I never really listened to real hard."

Vickers paused, his gaze searching Zak's face, his lips quivering slightly as if trying to form words, as if, for once, he was trying to summon reason to frame a question. "Walsh said you work for Crook. And President Grant. Is that true?"

"It is. And that must remain something unspoken between us."

"You saved Crook's life, I heard."

"Stories have a way of growing larger with time and the telling of them."

"You—You're the one. They call you the Shadow Rider. What Delacruz was trying to tell me. The horseman of the shadow, that's who you are. Zak Cody."

"What's in a name?" Zak said. "We have more important things to discuss, Vickers."

"I'm beginning to realize that. Sir."

"You don't have to call me 'sir,' Vickers. And I'm not going to pull rank on you. Unless you force me to. You lost two sentries tonight. If the Navajos had wanted to, they could have killed the other soldiers you left behind. With that fire, they made perfect targets."

"Yes, I know. Now. I can't figure that out."

"Have you ever heard of a Navajo named Narbona?"

"No, can't say as I have."

"Well, no matter. That's the leader of the bunch that stole those sheep from Gregorio Delacruz. And he made sure that Gregorio knew his name."

"Why?"

"I'm still trying to figure that out," Zak said.

"Is there a point to this, then?"

"Be patient, Vickers. I think Narbona was killed, or died, some years ago. The man who calls himself Narbona is too young to be the original."

"So, maybe his mother named him after the original Narbona."

Zak shook his head.

"The Navajos never say the name of one who has died. They never rename their children after a dead person."

"But—"

"But now we have another Narbona. The one who lived before gave Kearney and Kit Carson a great deal of trouble. He was revered by the entire Navajo nation. So now he's alive again. Or his namesake is. He amounts to something bigger than what we might expect."

"What do you mean?"

"I mean that *this* Narbona is a kind of ghost warrior, a man risen from the dead. I think this one is bent on reclaiming all the Navajo lands. And I think he has a plan to do just that."

Vickers was silent for a change. Zak could see that wheels and gears were turning in the man's mind. He hoped the impact of his statement, his assessment of Narbona, was sinking in deeply. He wanted Vickers to comprehend the gravity of the situation. He knew he was going to need an ally in this shadowy prelude to what might become a full-blown war. New Mexico had seen its share of troubles with the Navajo, and nobody in Washington or the territory wanted to see a return to those blood-soaked days when the Navajos raided, pillaged, and murdered many a settler.

Finally, Vickers broke his silence.

"I've got to warn Colonel Loomis. He'll want to go after this Narbona, nip his plan in the bud."

"I think that's exactly what Narbona hopes you will do, Vickers."

"Huh?"

"Can't you see it yet?" Zak asked.

"See what?"

"Narbona told Gregorio to tell the soldiers about what he did to his family and one of his sheepherders. Narbona wants the army to take to the field and come after him."

"Why?"

"So he can lead them into the Jemez and destroy the entire force stationed at the Presidio."

"Hell, Cody, Colonel Loomis would bring field artillery and blow him to kingdom come."

"Loomis would never get a howitzer anywhere near Narbona. Not in that country."

"Well, there has to be a way. Loomis is more than competent. He's a fighter."

"Right now, Vickers, I don't want Colonel Loomis to know about any of this."

"Sir, I'm bound to report all this to my commanding officer."

Zak sucked in a breath. They could hear the men talking in low tones. Some were grumbling about the late hour and the lack of sleep. Others were mourning the deaths of the two sentries, Kelso and Deming.

"Vickers, I ought to shoot you here where you now stand," Zak said.

"What did you say?" Vickers had his hackles up, Zak knew.

"You heard me, Vickers. I'm asking you to hold off on that report for a while. There are some things I want to check. I want to find out more about Narbona, track him, find out how much strength he has. That will take time and patience. You've heard of patience, haven't you?"

"Sir, I think I've had quite enough of your slanderous and demeaning remarks."

"Then, listen to me real careful, Vickers. If you report to Loomis what has happened this day and what I've told you about Narbona, you'll be responsible for the deaths of many men. Can you understand that?"

"I believe in the United States Army, not in some renegade with a dead man's name."

"I think it's a lot more than that, Vickers. Narbona probably has a sufficient number of men who know the country, who can hide in plain sight, and who can ambush any soldiers sent against him and defeat them. I also know that Narbona is getting help from people in Santa Fe. White men."

"Do you have any proof of that?"

"Not yet. That's why I need some time."

"I can't sit on this information forever, you know."

A small cloud passed under the moon and a brief shadow blotted out Vickers' face, but Zak knew the captain was right on that score.

"I need one man to go with me in the morning. One of your men, Vickers. I need someone who can live off the land, who can endure heat and hunger and thirst. Any suggestions?"

"You want me to volunteer?"

The cloud passed on and there was a pasty sheen to Vickers' face.

"No, you need to command and lead your men while I'm gone. Do not go back to Santa Fe until I return. Can you do that?"

"We're low on provisions ourselves."

"Don't try my patience too much, Vickers."

"Yes, I can do that. The only man I know who might be of help to you is Sergeant Bullard."

"What do you know about him?"

"He has a good record. He's fought Indians before. He's tough as an army boot and loyal as a bird dog."

"I'll take Bullard with me, then."

"How long do you expect to be gone?"

"Two days. Maybe three."

"Three days is a long time."

"Not when you weigh it against a war that could last years."

"I wish I could honor your prediction with credence," Vickers said.

"I'll put it to you this way, Captain. If I'm not back on the third day, you can ride to Santa Fe and tell Colonel Loomis anything you want. You can give him your report and your opinion and tell him that Zak Cody is a bag of wind. Fair enough?"

Vickers looked down at his feet. He dug a small furrow in the dirt with the toe of his boot, then looked up at Zak.

"Fair enough," he said.

Zak smiled.

"If you run out of meat, Vickers," he said, "you can buy a sheep or two from Gregorio."

"I—I . . ." Vickers was at a loss for words.

"I'll pay for the vittles," Zak said. Then he reached in his pocket and pulled out several folded bills. He slapped them into Vickers' hand, turned, and walked back to where the soldiers were starting to lie down on their bedrolls.

Vickers stood there, shaking his head. He looked down at the bills in his hand and then tucked them into his pocket.

"What manner of man is this?" he whispered to himself.

The seam along the eastern horizon parted, and gray light spilled through and spread across the sky. Zak and Sergeant Randy Bullard were already up, pouring hot coffee down their throats. By the time the sky was aflame with the dawn, the two were riding up the small canyon, their rifle butts resting on their pommels, the barrels pointing straight up like iron stakes. Zak pointed to the tracks from the day before, which were still evident, although filled with sand and grit.

The two men did not speak. Zak had briefed Bullard the night before and Randy seemed eager to follow Zak into the wilderness. They both carried full canteens and enough grub to last three days, if they didn't eat much.

They came to the place where Zak had found the sheep.

"Those sheepskins?" Randy asked.

"Narbona killed two sheep. I figure they made camp somewhere and cooked the meat."

"Or ate it raw."

Zak didn't laugh. It was plain to him that Bullard had his own opinions of Indians and nothing Zak could say would change his mind.

"You ever do any tracking, Randy?"

"Some. Not in country like this. It looks like somebody took a firebrand to it and burned it to a crisp."

"That's volcanic ash," Zak said.

"I see a lot of tracks. Horse and sheep and what looks like Injun mockersons."

"And what do they tell you?" Zak asked.

Bullard studied the ground. He rode his horse around in a circle, then returned to his starting point, next to Nox.

"Well, looks to me like they all scattered like a covey of bobwhites."

Zak smiled.

"They split up, all right. But Narbona wanted soldiers to come up here, find those sheep, and come after him."

"That what you think, Zak?"

"That's part of what I think. In some ways, it doesn't make sense. He didn't drive the sheep any farther than here. He and his men went their separate ways. Why?"

"Hell, I don't know."

"Neither do I, but I expect, if we look close enough, we'll find places up ahead where some of those men could hide and look right down here."

Bullard raised his head and gazed at the high ground, scanning every cone-shaped hill and rocky outcropping.

"Maybe someone's a-watchin' us now," Randy said.

"Maybe."

Zak rode out of the flat place and followed a pair of horse tracks that wound through small hills and strange formations—lumps of earth that were small and squat or head-high and round—that rose out of the ground in erratic patterns. Each was flecked with stones and rocks and scraggly plants that were so twisted and malformed, they seemed to have grown up in agony.

An hour's ride further, the two sets of tracks separated: one to the south; the other due west, through jumbles of small spires and coned hills that gave the landscape a look of desolation as far as the eye could see.

On either side of the horse tracks, larger hills began to appear as if to indicate there was much higher ground ahead. Yet, it seemed to Zak that they were in a kind of bowl, separated from the Sangre de Cristo range, as if the land had been permanently cut off from the main range in the far distant past. It became plain to him that the rider was following a trail, but not a heavily traveled one. It wasn't a game trail, because there were no animal tracks other than the horse's, and yet he could see some definition across the lava ash, a faint path less than a foot wide.

"How come you're follerin' this here track, 'stead of any of the others, Zak?"

The two men were sweating under the high sun. Their shadows were puddles ahead of them, but shrinking as the sun neared its zenith.

"Because the man riding the horse we're following is staying to open ground. He has nothing to worry about. He knows the country. He knows where he's going."

"What about the other'ns?" Bullard asked.

"Those might be the ones watching the back trail. Two of them left drops of blood on the ground. This is one of them."

"Huh? I didn't see no blood."

"Hard to see on that black ground. But those sheep were dripping blood. A while back, I saw a place where the rider who turned off to the south passed his sheep carcass to the other man. That's the man we're following."

Bullard stared hard at the ground. He saw unshod hoof scuffs and marks, but nothing else.

"You must have eyes like a damned eagle, Zak."

"You generally see what you're looking for."

"And you was lookin' for blood drops?"

"They cut the throats of those sheep and rode on. They let the sheep bleed out. They didn't gut them out or quarter them. So I don't think they were going far."

"You think we're getting close to that Injun camp?"

Zak didn't answer. There was no answer. In that country, what was close? What was far? It was a place that nature had forgotten, or perhaps had never known about. What had created the myriad of cone-shaped hills that looked like the caps of elves? What volcano had erupted and cloaked the soil with that black dust? What wind had swept through and wiped all but the most primitive life from its black surface?

As they rode, the land rose gradually. They were

gaining altitude, a few inches at a time, and the features were changing. Hills on the other side of them began to rise higher and grow broader and longer. They found themselves in a trackless, jumbled terrain that defied mapping and remembrance. There were no outstanding landmarks, no distinctive features that a man could remember passing in an hour, a day, or two days. There were no trees to blaze, no trail to mark for their return. There were only the faint tracks of an unshod horse with no definable destination.

An hour later, with the sun past its zenith and glaring into their faces, the tracks led up a narrow defile that looked like an old wash from an ancient flood. The defile rose up a slope, and they climbed a small hill and kept on to an even larger hill, and then reached a still larger mound with a slightly rounded top that took them into a cooler, slightly thinner atmosphere.

Zak called a halt and looked around. They were in the open and there was no cover for several hundred yards in any direction. They were surrounded by larger hills, and any one or all of them could harbor watchful men with rifles whose bullets could reach them. Off to the right, Zak spotted a cluster of large boulders.

Bullard pulled out a cigarette and a box of matches. He offered a Piedmont to Zak, who shook his head.

"You don't smoke," Randy said.

"It blocks the sense of smell."

"You ain't a dog, Zak. What do you need a sense of smell for?"

Zak smiled.

"Everything on this earth gives off a scent. Smelling something that can eat you could save your life."

"Never thought of it thataway."

Bullard lit up.

Zak studied the tracks. They were heading toward the strewn boulders, which formed a kind of bulwark to an open place that was barely visible. He sniffed the air: A faint mixture wafted from that rocky place—the scents of wood smoke and cooked mutton, the tang of urine and human feces.

While Bullard smoked, Zak scanned the terrain around them and saw an overturned pebble, a small furrow a few yards away, a faint hoofprint near a scuffed patch of soil.

He left Bullard there and rode in a wide circle, staring at the ground. He saw more tracks. Tracks going and coming. A dozen or so at first glance. He rode back to where Bullard was waiting and cocked his head toward the boulders.

"This is where the whole bunch came," he said. "Let's go where those boulders are. You take the right flank and I'll come in from the left side. Keep your thumb on that hammer."

"You think Injuns are behind them big rocks?"

"No, Randy. But you never know. Just go in slow and be ready to shoot."

Bullard ground out his cigarette on his saddle horn and stuck the remains in his shirt pocket. Zak rode off to the left. Bullard approached from the right.

The boulders formed a semicircle around the large, flat patch. Zak rode Nox in between two of the rocks and looked down at the ground.

Bullard came in from the other side. He let out a sigh of relief.

"Nary a soul here," the sergeant said.

"They ate their supper here," Zak said.

"I see bones and places where they sat."

"That fire ring is full of ashes."

"What did they burn? Ain't no trees real close."

"They carried in their wood," Zak said. "See that piece of scrub pine? It didn't burn all the way down."

"You're sayin' they got a camp up in the mountains?"

"Maybe more than one camp."

"You read a lot from just a few scraps, Zak."

"They were here less than two hours, I'd say. Pretty well organized. Look, from the front here, they can see the way we came up, and all around. They were safe here and they knew it."

"Yeah. Gives me a funny feelin'. Hell, they could have bunked here overnight and picked us off when we rode up."

"Easy as pie," Zak said.

Zak heard a far-off sound. Just a snick of a sound, but he knew what it meant.

"Get off your horse, Randy," he said. "Put him up flat against that big rock, and take cover."

Before Randy could react, Zak had dismounted and snubbed Nox up against another large boulder.

"What's up, Zak?"

Bullard crouched behind a smaller boulder next to the one where his horse stood.

"I heard someone cock a Henry or a Winchester."

"I never heard nothin'."

"Well, one of those two bucks came back here, or they left a lookout behind."

"Where?"

"Up on that next hill, I figure. Let's see."

Zak stripped his bandanna from around his neck and tied it to the end of his rifle. Then he poked the rifle barrel in between two boulders, shook it for a second, then quickly pulled it back out of sight.

A second later they heard the crack of a rifle. Both men ducked and a bullet struck the side of the boulder behind which Bullard was squatting. It caromed off the granite and whined off into space.

Bullard swore under his breath.

Zak untied the bandanna and stuffed it in his back pocket. Both horses whickered in fear, and Bullard's gelding pawed the ground. Bullard pulled on the reins to hold his horse's head down and prevent the animal from bolting.

"That trick won't work a second time," Zak said.

"What are we going to do? The bastard's got us pinned down."

Zak drew a breath and thought about the situation. Whoever had fired the shot knew he hadn't hit anyone. He could be moving in closer or taking up another position. The shooter could afford to wait them out.

Zak knew that he and Bullard could probably sneak off down the side of the hill they were on, gain a few minutes until they mounted up and rode like hell for cover. Or he might be able to draw another shot from the bushwhacker and see the muzzle flash. That would be dangerous, and might not work.

He looked at Bullard. The man was ready to

fight, but he was as blind as Zak was. They were pinned down behind the boulders. Safe, but unable to return fire to an enemy they could not see.

"Well?" Bullard asked again. "Any ideas, Zak?"

"I know one thing," Zak said.

"What's that?"

"We aren't going to surrender."

Another shot rang out and the bullet plowed a furrow between the two men. The shooter had aimed between the boulders and gotten through with a round.

That shot told Zak something.

The shooter had moved, or there was another one out there.

The last shot had been several yards closer. But how close?

Too damned close, Zak thought.

⊱ 10 ⊰

Zak knew that if he didn't act fast, the shooter would keep them pinned down until his reinforcements came. Then he and Bullard wouldn't have a chance in hell of getting out alive.

"Those shots came from a Spencer repeater," Zak said.

"I know. Might be one they took off'n Kelso or Deming."

"Randy, I want you to lie as flat as you can, put two rounds up there in the trees higher up on this hill. Think you can do that? Just shoot and duck back behind that boulder."

"What're you goin' to do?"

"I'm going to slip out and see if I can mark the muzzle flash, drop the shooter."

"You're takin' a big chance."

"So are you, Randy. Now, don't shoot until I get set and give you the high sign."

"Right," Bullard said.

Zak scooted over to an opening large enough for him to bolt through—to throw himself flat on the ground and look for that muzzle flash. He thumbed back the hammer on his Winchester, nodded toward Bullard.

Bullard rolled into the small opening, fired a shot into the scrub pines and junipers growing at the far end of the hill behind them. His rifle cracked, sounding like the snap of a bullwhip and the bullet sped toward the trees. He triggered off another shot and Zak hurled himself through the opening.

The man in the trees fired at Bullard. Zak saw the orange flash through a gap in the trees. The man was on horseback and was using a larger pine tree for cover.

Zak fired at the horse's rump, which stuck out, a brownish lump. The bullet struck the tree and sheared off a chunk of bark. The horse bucked forward and Zak saw the rider lower his rifle and fight to stay in the saddle. Then the rider turned and the horse started to gallop back up the slope and into thicker vegetation. Zak levered another cartridge into the chamber and fired a quick shot at the retreating rider. He heard the bullet smash through limbs and crack them into splinters. The hoofbeats sounded loud and then faded.

He lay there, jacked another bullet into the firing chamber, and listened.

Then he started scooting backwards, feeling his way through the opening in the boulders.

"Get him?" Bullard asked.

"I don't think so," Zak said.

"You got off a couple of shots. See the muzzle flash and all?"

"I did," Zak said. "And I saw the rider. Just for a moment."

"Navajo?"

"Well, if it was a Navajo, he was wearing an army uniform—a cavalry uniform—and he had on a campaign hat."

"The hell you say."

"Mount up and let's ride up there. I want to see those tracks and follow that jasper, whoever he is."

In seconds, the two men mounted their horses and rode toward the trees. They were ten yards apart and hunched over so that they didn't present their upper torsos to anyone who might still be waiting in ambush.

Zak studied the tracks and so did Bullard.

"That's mighty puzzlin' and perplexin'," Bullard said. "You might have been right, Zak."

"That's a shod horse that made those tracks. I did see a uniformed rider. And he was shooting a Spencer repeating rifle."

"Yep, he sure was."

Zak looked for blood spatter or droplets on the ground. He knew that he had missed the horse's rump and he was pretty sure he hadn't wounded the rider. The tracks showed that the horse was going away at a fast trot, zigzagging through the brush and scrub trees like a fleeing rabbit.

They rode over a small saddleback and into an even larger hill, one that came to a conical peak another thousand feet higher. But the tracks veered off and started skirting the hill, dropping off to their right. Then the going got rough, for the hillside was steep. Zak saw where the shod horse had dislodged dirt and rocks, slipped sideways a few inches, then climbed higher before going lower again. There were no trails there, and the brush was thick, the ground rocky and treacherous.

Zak and Randy came to a slide and saw where the rider had plunged his horse straight down.

"Reckless," Zak said, noticing the deep gouges the iron hooves had made as the horse braked and slid down on its rump. The slide ended in a thicket growing among three hillocks. They could both see the first dirt and rocks piled up, either wet and brown or smooth and gray, depending on which side was exposed to the sun.

"He got clean away," Bullard said.

Zak cupped his right ear and turned his head a few inches from left to right. He listened for sounds made by the horse, the click of an iron hoof on stone, the crunch of a bush or tree limb, the clatter of dislodged pebbles. All was quiet. All was unnerving in that silence.

"Hmmm." Zak turned his horse and rode back up to the hilltop. Bullard followed. As he rode, Zak stuffed two fresh cartridges into his rifle's magazine. He heard Bullard reloading the Spencer behind him.

"Now what?" Bullard asked when they reached the place where the sniper had fired upon them.

"Let's see if I can pick up tracks of the Navajos who ate those sheep. See if they split up or rode somewhere in a bunch."

"You're the tracker, Zak. All I see is ground we tore up ourselves."

Zak's jaw tightened for just a second. He thought of a phrase he had heard while serving in the army, scouting for General Crook, fighting Indians in the north and the far west. *When the pupil is ready, the teacher appears.* He didn't remember who said it, but the phrase had stuck with him. He thought

Randy Bullard might be ready to learn something about tracking, and there was no better time than the present.

"We'll ride through the moil of that bushwhacker's tracks and our own, Randy. We'll look for unshod hoof marks."

"You goin' to teach me a thing or two?"

"Maybe. You ride alongside me as much as you can and I'll try and show you how to read the ground."

"Fair enough, Zak. Where'd you learn all this?"

"From the Sioux, the Cheyenne, the Blackfeet, the Pawnee."

"You been over the road, ain't you?"

Zak rode on into the brush, his leg brushing against the scrub pines, limbs from a small juniper scraping Nox's leg.

"You look at unmarked ground. Keep that picture in your mind. Then you look for a scuff mark, some little mark that seems out of place. Like there."

Zak pointed to the ground.

"Yeah, looks like . . . well, I don't know what it looks like. It ain't got no clear . . . what do you call it?"

"Definition."

"Yeah, it ain't got that."

"The dirt has filled in something that was there. A hoof mark, a gouge. Wind may have pushed dirt into the track. But it's a track. Now, you follow that and look for more signs. Every so often you'll see a clear track. It might be blurred by falling dirt that built up along the sides, but it'll be clear enough."

"I see one," Bullard said. "And another'n right close to it."

"Now, let your eyes roam over on both sides of it. A few feet each way. You might see more marks or tracks, disturbed soil."

Zak smiled as Bullard passed him, his gaze locked to the ground. He was like a bloodhound on the scent. There were more tracks and Bullard was finding them, eager as a kid following the blood trail of his first deer.

Zak showed him how to look for bent branches, bruised blades of grass, a slightly dislodged pebble. All were signs of some walking creature having disturbed the natural order of the terrain. Bullard was an eager student and he began to notice things he would usually overlook.

"So, the Injuns taught you to track. But how did they do it? Like we're a-doin'?" Bullard was curious. A good sign, Zak thought.

"We walked game trails, followed buffalo herds, looked at places where quail had dusted their feathers. They showed me tracks in snow and on sand. Sometimes they had me just sit in one spot and watch a small patch of ground for half a day or more. I watched ants, grasshoppers, doodlebugs, ticks on trees and leaves. I looked at small creatures until I could track an ant across a rock."

"Really?"

"Almost," Zak said, with a wry smile.

They came to a game trail less than a foot wide. There were deer tracks and horse tracks, bird tracks and rabbit droppings. The trail led deeper into the hills and mountains, and they saw a variety of plants: cactus, ocotillo, grass and sage, different kinds of trees. And the land began to break up into small ravines and washed-out gullies, little hills and bigger hills, a crazy quilt of patterns and designs that became bewildering passageways into a strange world, the world of the Navajo.

The horses they were tracking had broken up, all going separate ways.

"We won't follow tracks anymore today," Zak said. "It's too slow and taxing."

"What now?" Bullard asked.

"Take to the high ground. See how far we can see. Move slow and listen. Smell. That's part of tracking, too."

"It is? How so?"

"These Navajos are already trying to hide their tracks, or didn't you notice?"

"You mean all them flat rocks buried in the ground, the hardpan we crossed."

"Yes. They don't want anyone following them to wherever they're going."

"But you don't know where they're headed, huh?"

"I don't know the exact place, but I might know the kind of place," Zak said.

"What kind of place?" Bullard studied Zak's face. Zak's hat brim shaded most of it, and there was a slash of light across his mouth and chin. His eyes were dark vacancies, sunk in shadow.

"A safe place where they keep their women and kids. A place where they can grow corn and tend sheep. A place that can be defended with only a few men. A place where they can go in one way and out another."

"You mean like a canyon?"

"A box canyon, maybe," Zak said, "open on both ends. Or maybe several canyons converging on a valley."

"We ain't seen nothin' like that so far."

"No, but we've been climbing gradually for the past two hours or so. And that sun is falling away in the sky. Dusk comes early in the mountains. The watch you carry in your pocket is no good up here."

"I reckon," Bullard said.

They climbed to high ground, crossed a narrow ridge and dropped down into a saddleback ravine, then continued on to another peak and crossed still another ridge. On either side were broken terrain, gullies and washes, small hills, and dry creek beds.

Near sunset, Zak rode across a narrow, tree-choked ridge and stopped suddenly, Bullard right behind him.

"See somethin'?" Bullard whispered, his senses suddenly alert.

"No," Zak said, "but there's a steep drop-off just ahead and I smell wood smoke."

Bullard raised his head slightly and sniffed. "I don't smell nothin'," he said.

Zak held up a hand. Then he cupped his right ear. He turned his head toward the drop-off.

Bullard sniffed a few more times.

"Listen," Zak whispered.

The slight breeze was blowing in circles. Shifting, changing, as if the currents were uncertain at that altitude. Zak figured they were at about nine or ten thousand feet above sea level.

Bullard started nodding.

They both heard snatches of voices. Voices that faded and became almost inaudible then vanished.

Zak signaled to Bullard to dismount. He climbed out of the saddle. He tied Nox to a small pine tree, gestured for Bullard to do the same. Then the two crept up to the drop-off, both hunched over like cats stalking a bird or a squirrel.

They squatted at the edge and looked down. There was a wide valley below them. Smoke rose in the sky and turned to tangled cobwebs once it reached the draft blowing through. There were canyons on both sides, and they saw hogans and horses and heard children's laughter, the shrill high-pitched voices of women, the faint *tink* of a wooden spoon on a clay bowl, the bleating of sheep. And at the far end were small fields with corn planted in clumps, the stalks knee-high, and tree stakes where beans climbed in spirals and jiggled in the breeze.

Men rode in and out of both ends of the canyon on unshod horses, and there were men smoking in front of their hogans or washing their faces in the small creek that threaded through the valley like a small silver snake.

Bullard's mouth dropped open and his eyes widened.

"That's their damned camp," he breathed.

"One of them, anyway," Zak said, and he knew that every minute they stayed where they were, they were in danger.

He made a quick count of the men he could see.

It was not a small camp. And it had been occupied for some time. He counted more than fifty men, and then froze.

One of them was looking up toward them, shading his eyes from the sun. It seemed to Zak that the Navajo warrior was not only looking at him, but straight into his eyes.

He clamped a hand on Bullard's arm.

"Don't move," he said. "Don't even breathe."

The Navajo brave, a statue, naked except for a breechcloth and moccasins, continued to stare straight at them.

As if the man knew they were there.

11

The Navajo brave down in the valley pointed to the ledge and began yelling something in his native tongue.

"Move," Zak said, scooting backward, away from his perch.

Bullard wriggled to get out of sight of the Navajo camp.

"Let's light a shuck," Zak said, running to his horse. He swung up into the saddle. A moment later Bullard was mounted, and the two rode into the trees and headed downslope.

"Where to?" Bullard asked.

"Just follow me, Randy."

Zak picked his trail, weaving in and out of trees and passing over hardpan when he could, nosing Nox through heavy brush and over small boulders, putting spurs to him when there was enough open space to run. The sun sank over the western rim of the Sangre de Cristos and beyond the Jemez, burning the last daylight in the sky, rimming the red-smeared clouds with silver and gold. Its yellow light turned the azure sky to a pale blue-green pastel as it spread out in a wide fan to mix the colors.

Both men were panting. Sweat oiled their faces, soaked through their clothes. The horses were not lathered, but their hides were slick with perspiration. Zak wheeled Nox into an aperture between two low ridges, turned into a shallow gully filled with rocks and brush. He reined up and scanned his surroundings.

They were protected from direct rifle fire as long as they stayed in the gully, and nobody could approach from either end without being seen. It was not a good spot for a long siege, but it would serve as a temporary place to rest. More than that, the acoustics were perfect. He could hear someone coming on horseback or foot from some distance away, where they were.

"We stayin' here?" Randy asked, his sides heaving, his breathing deep and labored from the exertion.

"We might lay up here until the sun goes down," Zak said.

"Good. I'm out of breath."

"Just listen for a while, Randy. Listen real hard."

The horses stood hipshot, catching their breaths. Sweat striped their coats, trickled down their legs, dripped from their fetlocks. Flies swarmed for the fresh, salty liquid, and the breeze that had cooled them as they rode died out in that sunken bowl, turning it into a steam bath.

The two men listened for several minutes. They heard neither human voices nor the sound of hoofbeats. A red-tailed hawk flew over, dragging its corrugated shadow along one of the ravine walls, then floated out of sight without making a sound. The silence rose up around them and enveloped them. They began to breathe in regular, smooth breaths as they both wiped sweat from their foreheads, faces, and necks. The horses did not show signs of alarm; Zak was watching both of them, looking at their ears, which were more powerful than his own.

Bullard pulled out his pack of cigarettes and was just about to shake one out and stick it between his lips when both men straightened up as if their spines had turned to ramrods. Both horses brought up their heads and their ears stiffened to hard cones and began to twist toward the sound.

Zak heard the clank of an iron hoof on stone, then a cascade of falling rocks less than fifty yards from them. From another direction, there was the sound of many hoofbeats. These were muffled, with no clang of metal against stone.

Both men craned their necks to peer out of the gully. Bullard stood up in his stirrups.

A rider halted his horse and waited there in plain view while the sounds of the unshod horses grew louder. A few seconds later the halted rider was surrounded by several Navajos, all buck naked except for breechcloths and moccasins.

The lone rider on the shod horse was wearing an army uniform, a billed campaign hat tight on his head. His Spencer jutted out of his boot. He started signing with his hands and Zak heard snatches of disconnected Spanish words. One of the Navajos also spoke in Spanish.

The meeting did not last long. The soldier turned his horse and rode back toward the valley of the Rio Grande. All of the Navajos, a dozen or more, followed after him.

"That horse the soldier was riding was a bay mare," Zak said. "Just like the one I shot at up in those trees."

"It sure was. And I recognized the trooper," Bullard said. He licked dry lips. "About swallered my own throat. A fucking traitor."

"The soldier was a Mexican," Zak said.

"Sure was. That was Sergeant Renaldo Dominguez. Good old Naldo, the sonofabitch."

Zak said nothing. His eyes narrowed to slits as the sounds of the riders faded away and the land settled back into silence.

Shadows crawled down the sides of the ravine, filled the gully.

They heard more horses pass by, within fifty yards, following the same course as the previous riders.

"I wonder what Naldo's up to, what he told them redskins," Bullard said when it grew quiet again.

"We can't risk finding out right now," Zak said.

"We goin' to stay here?"

"No, but we'll have to find a safe place to spend the night."

"Hell, it's practically night already."

"Don't light up any cigarettes, Randy. We'll go out the other end, walk our horses real slow and find a spot to lay out our bedrolls."

"I don't cotton much to stayin' out here all night."

"It might be the safest place."

They waited another hour, until it was pitch dark. Then they made their way slowly out of the tangle of brush and climbed back onto flatter land. Zak looked at the stars and got his bearings, then proceeded to follow a ridge down onto a wide, flat place that was dotted with conical hills, cactus, and lava dust.

They stopped often to listen, but widened the distance between them and the gully, wending ever eastward and holding close to the higher hills. Zak saw a promising configuration and rode up a slope to the top of a ridge. Hills surrounded them like the shadows of giant reptiles, snaking in and out of lesser hills, flat terrain, and higher peaks. It was like riding through a deserted landscape in another world. They could not see far, and so relied on the horses to pick their way along the ridgeline.

They found a cluster of scrub pines and gnarled juniper bushes and Zak reined up. He rode around the place and looked at it from every angle.

"This might be good," he said. "No reason for a Navajo to ride up here, and if we stay in the trees, we can't be seen by anybody riding below on either side of us."

"What about the horses?"

"We'll grain and water them just enough so that they won't grumble about it much," Zak said.

"Unsaddle 'em?"

"No. We might have to leave in a hurry. No hobbles, either."

"All right," Bullard said. "Wish I could smoke, though."

"Tomorrow," Zak said.

They tied the horses apart from each other, at either end of the tree cover.

Bullard laid out his bedroll after brushing away rocks to smooth the ground where he lay his blanket. Zak laid his sleeping gear out near Nox at the opposite end of the copse of trees, kicking rocks out of the way and scraping the ground free of small stones.

"It's awful quiet up here," Bullard said.

"We'll stand watches. I'll take the first. You get some sleep."

"I'll try. I keep thinkin' of all them redskins we saw. They's only two of us and God knows how many Injuns."

"Don't worry about them, Randy. They're not worried about us. Get some shut-eye."

Bullard took off his hat and stripped off his gun belt. He laid his Spencer next to his blanket and lay down.

In a few minutes, he was asleep.

Zak sat down with his rifle, the trees at his back. He looked at the stars and chewed on a piece of hardtack, washed the mass down with water from his canteen.

He had spent many such nights in the wilderness, out on the plains, up in the Rockies. He enjoyed the solitude and the stars, the vast expanse of the night sky, and when the moon rose, he looked down on a mysterious world of strange shapes and undecipherable shadows. The night land had its own rhythms and pulses. Creatures moved about, hunting, sniffing, listening, and he felt a part of that world.

He thought of Naldo Dominguez, a sergeant in the U.S. Army, now a deserter, or at least in cahoots with Narbona and the renegade Navajos. What was his mission? Why would a man give up his duty as a soldier and join such an enemy? What was behind all the predations along the Rio Grande, and the two white men who had been with Narbona and then gone into Santa Fe? There seemed no sense to any of it.

But Zak knew that everything made sense, eventually.

A man had to figure it out, no matter how puzzling it all seemed.

But this was something he had never encountered before. This was Navajo land, and it held many mysteries.

How could an army, a troop of cavalrymen, go up against such enemies? This was not the plains or the mountains. Here, the enemy could melt away in a thousand mazes and leave no track. Worse, the enemy had no clear face. It was a mix of races and faces. If it came to a fight, army against army, where was the battlefield? Who was the enemy?

Who *was* the enemy?

That was the question.

12

Randy stood at Zak's feet, nudging the sole of Zak's boot with his toe. Zak awoke immediately, threw off his blanket, and sat up. It was still dark, but Zak knew that it was close to dawn. The chill breath of a breeze blew at his face, seeped through his clothing to his skin. He grabbed his rifle and stood, adjusting his eyes to the moonlit darkness, the star sheen gleaming like liquid metal on the bill of Bullard's cap.

"Report," Zak whispered. Sometimes the military in him came to the forefront. This was one of those times, he realized.

"Sir, I didn't know how far sound could travel at night. Out here, I mean. This is a good outpost. I heard riders way off."

"Any of them come close?"

"No, but I heard activity. Couldn't tell exactly where the noises was comin' from, but I heard a lot of horses. Goin' west, up into the hills where we was yesterday. Up to that Navajo camp."

"Did you eat?"

"I sure did, Zak. Gnawed through hardtack and jerky, gobbled down a cup of rancid beans."

Zak suppressed a laugh.

"How long ago did you hear the horses?"

"A while after I took over your watch. Maybe an hour later. Sounded like they was all strung out."

"No talk?"

"Didn't hear none."

"So, the Navajos and Sergeant Dominguez went somewhere and came back. A raid?"

"Maybe," Bullard said.

"Might be safe for us to ride down to the valley and see what Captain Vickers has to say."

"You're the boss, Zak."

"I'll ride down first, then give a whistle if it's clear. You wait up here. You hear anything, you give me a whistle."

Zak rode down to the flat. He dismounted, put his ear to the ground. He heard nothing. He whistled, then climbed back up in the saddle.

He waited for Bullard to join him, then rode to the east, following the easiest path through hills and mounds, stopping every so often to listen. It was still cool and there was a slight breeze blowing down from the mountains at their backs. The horses were frisky and stepped out well on the volcanic dust, their hooves landing solid on the hardpan. They would leave tracks, Zak knew, but that was unavoidable. It was still full dark, but he could feel the dawn flexing its muscles just below the horizon. He wanted to get back to the old camp before the sun rose high enough to strike them full in their faces. They rode out of the jumble of hills and he knew they were making good time on the downhill ride to the valley.

The moon paled to a ghost and the stars faded

in a sky filling with light. Dawn broke across a rusty horizon that opened up like a wound, gushing blood, gold, and silver onto the far cloudbanks. The cool freshets of air from the mountains retreated as the heat advanced across the majestic land, stagelit to life with a suddenness that took a man's breath away.

Zak pulled the brim of his hat down and lowered his head into its shade. He touched the beard stubble on his chin and rubbed the short hairs so that it sounded like sandpaper gliding across a chunk of wood. They came onto the plain and the tracks of unshod horses stood out like dimples in a pudding. Tracks from the west revealed a shod horse among them. But there were tracks going the other way, too, and Zak felt something tighten in the back of his brain, the worm of a thought inching up as he saw the return tracks, those heading back up into the wild reaches. These were threaded with shod horses, horses carrying little weight, hieroglyphs of iron hooves in the dirt and sand.

Bullard saw the stirred-up earth, but did not decipher the scrawled tracks that were etched in the earthen tablet.

"Lots of tracks," Bullard said. "Wonder if the boys chased them Injuns off. Looks like they was prowlin' close to where we had our camp."

"It's worse than that, Randy," Zak said. There were steel bands in his stomach and they tightened down on his gut as if some hand was wrapping them around an iron barrel.

In the distance Zak saw the smoke from Santa Fe, tendrils rising into the bluing sky, fanning out as they reached the upper air lofts. Below, the valley was still in shadow, a dim jumble of rocks and cactus, thin sentinels of ocotillo, and the coarse brown rust of centuries. Beyond, the river turned to a multicolored sash that flexed like a snake swallowing its young.

"I think I see that bunch of rocks where we camped," Bullard said.

They rode over a moil of horse tracks and Zak felt something catch in his chest, as if a force was squeezing his heart.

"You don't get it, do you, Randy?" Zak said.

"Get what?"

"You see any horses down there? Any sign of life?"

Randy stood up in his stirrups as if he were riding a jumper.

"Well, no, not yet," he said.

"Better brace yourself. You might not like what you see on the other side of those rocks."

The two rode down and circled the rocks. Bullard gasped when he saw the naked bodies sprawled on the ground like broken dolls. His horse snorted and backed down on its haunches. Zak rode up and gazed down on the dead men.

Each man had been stripped of his clothes and boots. There were no rifles, no pistols. Even their bedrolls were gone.

Corporal Larry Mead and Corporal Stu Davis had their throats cut, their genitals stuffed in their open mouths. Lieutenant Walsh had been shot in the back. His throat was slit from ear to ear and he lay on his side, his eyes closed.

Bullard made a sound and when Zak turned to look at him, the sergeant was leaning to one side, vomiting a mixture of hardtack gruel and bits of dried beef onto the ground. His horse sidled away from the vomit, sidestepping as if he were on parade.

Zak tried to put the pieces together. It was not difficult to reconstruct what had happened.

But he wanted to make sure. He dismounted and walked over the blood-soaked ground, looking at the impressions their blankets had left, the smoothness of the earth with ripples and folds made by cloth and the weight of the men. He saw that Kelso and Deming also had been stripped of their clothes and weapons. There were brass shells lying about and he left them where they lay, but marked their positions. He sorted through the boot tracks and the moccasin tracks. He traveled back through time, uncovering everything, pulling up the evidence layer by layer until a picture began to form in his mind.

Bullard was still retching, but had dismounted. He was doubled over, the reins still in his hand.

Zak counted the bodies for the fourth time.

There were two men missing.

One of them was Sergeant Dominguez. Zak deduced that he had shot Walsh and the two corporals as they slept, then rode up into the hills to get the Navajos, bring them back down to attack the campsite, steal the horses, strip the dead of their clothing and weapons.

Bullard stood up, wiped his mouth. He dropped the reins and walked over to Zak.

"They're all dead, ain't they?"

"No, not all of them. Two are still alive."

Bullard swept the scene with a penetrating gaze.

"They all look dead to me," he said.

"These men are dead. Two are not."

"Yeah, Naldo ain't here. But we know where he is. Or where he went, that damned traitor."

"Captain Vickers is not here, either," Zak said.

Bullard looked at the obscene bodies of the dead men again. He squinched his eyes shut, then opened them. They were brimming with tears.

"No, he ain't here, is he?"

"We can scout around, waste our time," Zak said. "But I think Vickers wasn't here when all this happened."

"Where was he?"

"I don't know. Maybe riding off by himself, planning to move camp. No, he wasn't here—or he would be dead. I think he saw what happened, though. Or he came back after Dominguez left and saw his men lying dead here."

"Then, you think he took off after Naldo?"

"No. I think he knew something was very wrong and he pointed his horse toward Santa Fe."

"Sounds like Vickers."

"A man doing his duty. The way he sees it."

"Yeah, that would be Cap'n Vickers."

"I think we'll find him at the Presidio, reporting this massacre to Colonel Loomis."

"I think you might be right, Zak."

"You finished upchucking, Randy?"

"I'm empty as a gourd."

"Then let's get out of here, head for Santa Fe. We should be there by noon if we hurry."

The sun was up, blazing full bore across the land. They rode with the molten light square in their faces, putting their horses to the gallop on good ground, varying their pace. They crossed the river and headed for the town, which lay like something constructed from a dream, a village made of adobe and surrounded by hills and the ghosts of dead men, past and present.

In their wake, up in the rocks, the flies and the worms were busy reclaiming human flesh, reducing what had once been strong men to swollen caricatures soon to be lost from time and history.

Zak thought of them as he rode, and thought of the puzzle that had become so complex. He wondered if he, or anyone, could ever break the code.

Was there a solution to this particular enigma?

There were no answers yet.

There were only more questions, and each one burned like a hot coal in the furnace of Zak's mind. And deep down, beyond his reach, beyond his comprehension, something else was being forged in that furnace.

Hatred. A hatred for men who had no regard for life.

And hatred was a dangerous state of mind for a man. Hatred could cloud a man's judgment, blind him to reason.

Still, Zak could not push it back down, that hatred. It was focused not on the traitor, Dominguez. He was a mere pawn. Instead, the man Zak hated was some kind of ghost, a warrior that should never have been resurrected from the grave.

That man was Narbona.

═ 13 ═

Lieutenant Colonel Jeremiah Loomis towered over Captain Jeffrey Vickers. The two men together looked like figures in a recruiting picture for the United States Cavalry. Vickers had shaved, bathed, and donned a fresh, newly pressed uniform, and Loomis was spit and polish all the way, a West Pointer complete with swagger stick and a constant drumroll at the back of his strict military mind.

Loomis read the document Zak had handed him. He and Vickers stood next to the large cherry-wood desk in the commandant's office, both stiff as twelve-inch whipsawed boards.

"I was about to issue an arrest order for you, Cody. Captain Vickers expressed the opinion that you might have been a party to inciting the Navajos along the Rio Grande, inciting them to murder and rob our great citizens."

"I believe I was mistaken," Vickers said. "When I saw Sergeant Dominguez murder my boys, then ride off into the hills, I thought he was joining Cody and Bullard. Those two were gone by the time I awoke that morning. I was riding down to the river when I heard the shots. I saw Dominguez ride off.

When I saw the dead troopers I knew I had to ride here and get help."

"Cody," Loomis said, "this whole business is highly irregular. You don't wear a uniform. You do not report to any local superior officer. What am I to make of you? I have a wagon outside ready to go and pick up those dead troopers under Captain Vickers' command, and you're telling me not to take my troops to the field and kill or arrest those responsible."

"I believe, Colonel," Zak said, "that that is exactly why those soldiers were murdered. I also believe that the Navajo predations along the Rio Grande are part of that same scheme: to draw the army out into the field so that they can be slaughtered."

"Slaughtered? These are fighting men under my command here at Fort Marcy, and you're talking about a few renegade Navajos running around in small bands, disrupting the lives of innocent ranchers and farmers."

Sergeant Bullard stood at rigid attention just behind Zak, beads of sweat bleeding from the creases in his forehead. He cleared his throat in a loud rasp of air and both Vickers and Loomis stared at him as if he had just let out an explosive fart. Vickers frowned. Loomis crinkled his nose like a curious dog on the scent.

"Did you have something to say, Sergeant?" Loomis said.

"Well, sir, if you want to hear what I got to say."

"Speak up, man. Does your information pertain to the subject at hand?"

It took Bullard a second or two to digest and simplify the colonel's question.

"Maybe, sir," he said. "Me'n Zak, I mean Colonel Cody, was up in that country, lookin' down at that Navajo camp. They ain't no way to get in there after 'em without losin' a lot of men."

"Explain yourself, Sergeant," Loomis said.

"Well, sir, the whole country is all jumbled up, with hundreds of hills and canyons runnin' ever' whichaway, and so many places for Injuns to hide and such. You go in there with cavalry and you'd be ridin' right into a death trap."

Loomis turned his attention to Zak.

"That so, Cody?" Loomis, although he was outranked, still treated Zak like a civilian. The tone and the address was not lost on Zak, but he ignored it.

"It's a labyrinth in the Jemez, sir," he said with deliberate politeness. "I think there's more than one village in there. We saw only one, but I saw things there that led me to believe there are more just like it. And I counted fifty braves. Actually, it was what I didn't see that leads me to that conclusion."

"What do you mean by that, Cody—what you didn't see?"

"I didn't see a lot of horses, for one thing. I saw women and children, for another. It was not a war camp. But there were a lot of canyons feeding into it. It looked like the hub of a wheel, with spokes going out in all directions."

"How long did you observe this Navajo camp, Cody? Two minutes? Three? Five?"

"Less than five, probably."

Bullard cleared his throat again, but Loomis ignored him.

Loomis walked over to the window and looked out at the adobe blockhouse, the earthworks. Fort Marcy had been closed for some time and was just newly reopened. It was very near the Presidio, and was a conglomeration of adobe earthworks surrounded by a dry moat. Loomis was there on temporary duty until the government appointed a permanent commandant. He had hated the Presidio, and in spite of all the fort's homeliness, he was glad to have a place that was separate from the local government, the palace, and all the strings attached.

He turned and walked over to stand in front of Zak.

"You make a lot of assumptions on very little evidence, Cody."

"Yes, sir."

Loomis handed the document with Zak's assignment written on it back to him.

"According to this, you outrank me. But, I'm in charge of Fort Marcy and all the troops consigned to this post. Do you understand that?"

"I do, sir," Zak said.

Loomis walked back over to stand beside his desk, next to Vickers.

"Just so we understand each other. My duty is to go after renegades, Indian or white, to protect this city and this state."

Loomis paused, expecting some kind of response from Zak. Zak stood there, with no expression on his unshaven face. Sunlight streamed through the windows, but it was still cool inside the thick walls of the office. The sounds of marching men droned in the background, and a blacksmith's hammer clanged against an iron anvil. A horse whickered and men rattled leather traces as they lined up horses in harness just below Loomis's window.

"Just what is it you want me to do, Cody? In line with your assignment only, that is."

"Sir, I'd like a week to do some detective work here in Santa Fe. I would ask that you not take troops into the field until I have more information about what you might be facing if you go after the Navajos."

"A week? Out of the question." Loomis's voice was stern. "It'll take a day or so to get those dead troopers back here and buried with full military honors. Then I intend to take up the pursuit of this band of renegade Indians. I'll give you two days."

"Three," Zak said. "And do you remember the name of the Navajo leader I gave you earlier?"

"Yes, and as you suggested, I did some checking. Narbona, the Navajo who fought against Colonel Washington and Major Carson, was in his eighties back in forty-nine. He's long dead. So the man you say is leading these outlaws is an imposter."

"I'm sure he is, sir, since the Navajos never use the name of a dead man, or even say it aloud or in their thoughts after he is buried. But . . ."

"But what?"

"I think the Navajos might believe that the old Narbona, the one who died back in the fifties, has come back to life. They might believe this Narbona has returned to lead his people to victory, to reclaim former Navajo land."

"That's preposterous," Loomis said.

"But likely," Zak said.

Vickers looked as if he had been kicked square in the balls. His face drained of color and his neck veins swelled out until his skin crawled with blue worms.

"Three days," Loomis said. "I'll give you three days. May I ask what you intend to do in Santa Fe, what course your investigation will take?"

"I'm not at liberty to say, Colonel."

"Not at liberty to say? Sir, I demand you tell me what you plan to do in Santa Fe."

"Don't force me to pull rank on you, Colonel." Zak's jaw tightened and there was a ripple of flesh along his jawline. His eyes turned to hard flint and he skewered Loomis with the intensity of his gaze.

"Why, I ought to have you clapped in irons and thrown in the guardhouse for that remark."

"Nevertheless, sir, I do not want the details of my mission here to leak out. And I have one more request."

"And what is that, Mr. Cody?" Loomis was fighting to control his rage. He flexed his fingers and did everything he could not to ball them up into fists.

"I'll need a man to come with me. A cavalryman. But he must wear civilian clothes."

"Why, take Sergeant Bullard with you. Hell, you've already made a damned conscript of him."

"No, not Sergeant Bullard, although he's a brave and capable soldier. The man I need is one who will respect my rank, take orders, and later go into the field with full knowledge of what he's up against. I need a man who can command troops, an officer."

"I can't assign one of my officers to you for a mission I know nothing about, Cody."

"Sir, I'm not asking you," Zak said. "I'm telling you. I know who I want and I expect you to order that man to serve with me for those three critical days."

Loomis seemed about to have a fit of apoplexy. Vickers continued to scowl with all the facial movement of a cigar-store Indian. He was wooden and stiff, but it was plain that he half enjoyed seeing his commandant's feet put to the fire.

"Damn you, Cody. You're pushing your luck here. I could still have you thrown in the guardhouse."

"You could, and I'm sure you'd hear from General Crook or President Grant, either of whom would cheerfully strip you of all rank and consign you to hard labor at Fort Leavenworth."

"That sounds like a damned threat to me, Cody."

"It's good advice, Colonel. But take it any way you want to."

"An officer? You want an officer to go, ah, undercover with you? For three days only?"

"That's right."

"Well, I'd have to go over the roster, see who might be suited for such an unusual assignment."

"No, Colonel," Zak said, "you don't have to do that. I know the man I want."

All of the breath seemed to go out of Loomis. He still stood straight and tall, but he seemed unable to draw a breath or let one out.

"Well, who the hell is it?" Loomis said when he was able to get breath back in his lungs to push out the words.

"Captain Vickers."

"Me?" Vickers said.

"Yes, you," Zak said. "I trust you and I know you're the man who will use the information we obtain most wisely."

"Why, why . . ." Loomis spluttered.

"No arguments, Colonel Loomis," Zak said. "I'm the man they told you about at West Point."

"Huh, what's that? What do you mean, Cody?"

"That's Colonel Cody to you, sir. And I'm your superior officer."

Loomis looked like a man whirling on a spit over an open fire.

"Come on, Jeff," Zak said. "You and I have some work to do."

Vickers looked at Loomis.

"Oh, go on, Captain. Both of you, all three of you, get the hell out of here. Three days, Colonel Cody. Three days."

Loomis didn't shout, but he wanted to. Now his hands *did* ball up into fists, and sweat streamed over his face like the squeezings from a sour lemon.

Bullard saluted as Zak and Vickers left the room, their boots drumming on the thin hardwood floor.

"Sergeant," Loomis said. "Dismissed. Get a shave and take a bath before the stableman sweeps you out with the other horseshit."

"Yes, sir," Bullard said. He saluted and marched out of the room, leaving Colonel Loomis to ponder his own sanity and think fondly of a desk job back in Washington, D.C.

↦ 14 ↤

The transformation of Captain Jeffrey Vickers from soldier to civilian took less than an hour. That hour must have seemed like a month to Vickers, who wound up with a set of ill-fitting clothes, a battered hat, and a converted Remington New Model Army .44 that replaced his army-issue sidearm. The sutler found him a horse without a U.S. brand on its hip, a six-year-old, moth-eaten gelding with its ribs showing like barrel slats.

Zak suppressed the urge to laugh as the two rode out of Fort Marcy and past the Presidio. Vickers was plainly uncomfortable, but he no longer looked like a soldier. Instead, he looked like a derelict from some hellhole of a prison. Zak had seen to that, forcing Vickers to stand still while he threw parade ground dirt on his hat, shirt, trousers, and boots to complete the image he was looking for. As for Zak himself, he had neither shaved nor bathed, and the dust on his own person was legitimate and equally unbecoming.

"Just what is the purpose of us looking like a pair of outcasts?" Vickers said as they rode down a back street with very little traffic.

A pair of chickens waddled across the street in front of them. Vendors sat in front of adobe buildings displaying their wares: blankets, beads, clay pots, ollas, sombreros, serapes, leather sandals, saddles, knives, trinkets, and silver jewelry. This was Calle Once, several blocks from the town square, with its cantinas and cafés, its higher-class vendors and traders.

"You ever spend much time in a saloon, Vickers?"

"Not much. Why?"

"Do you know where Biederman's is?"

"The mercantile or the saloon?"

"Both," Zak said.

"Leo Biederman owns that whole block. I've never been in either of his establishments. But I understand he owns several businesses in Santa Fe. He's quite well respected, from what I hear."

"Do you know the man?"

"No, can't say as I do. I've seen him at the palace, in the Presidio a few times. From a distance."

"Think he'd recognize you?" Zak asked.

Vickers laughed.

"Not in this outfit, he wouldn't. I have had no dealings with the man. I doubt he knows that I exist."

"Good."

"Is that where we're going? To see Biederman?"

"Captain, what's the first thing you do when you're ordered into strange territory? You have no map, no guide, no knowledge whatsoever of who or where the enemy might be."

Vickers thought about the question for a couple of seconds.

"Reconnoiter would be the first order of the day."

Zak smiled.

"Well, that's what you and I are going to do. Reconnoiter. We're actors on a stage. We don't have anything to do with the army. We're civilians. We're men looking for a job and we don't care if the job is legal or not. We're just about flat broke and we'll do anything for gold or silver. Got that?"

"Got that, Zak."

"Now, you lead us to that saloon of Biederman's, Jeff. And keep your ears open for a couple of names we might hear."

"So, you do know something about the territory."

"Just the two names. One's Pete. The other's Ralph. Ever hear tell of anybody connected to Biederman with those two names?"

"First I've ever heard of those two. No last names?"

"No," Zak said.

Vickers turned down a street and headed toward the river and the mountains. Santa Fe was a collection of adobe huts, small buildings that seemed to have been constructed at different times. The clay bricks were dark or light, and there were even variations within single buildings. Some were houses, others little *tiendas*. There was a mixture of Mexicans, Americans, and Indians on every street. Some pushed small carts laden with woven blankets dyed in brilliant colors—red, green, yellow, blue, and brown. There were burros pulling *carretas* and children selling tobacco and homemade liquor, both amber and colorless. And there were dogs and cats and goats on tethers, all streaming through the little dirt streets.

"Any hotels near that cantina?" Zak asked as

they headed down Calle Esperanza, a street where the vendors sold flowers, seeds, squash, corn, tomatoes, beans, chilies, and other fruits and vegetables. The aromas were a change from the other streets they'd passed through, a mixture of earthy scents and aromatic herbs, tangy perfumes, and heady blossoms.

"Seems to me there are a couple of hotels on that same street, Calle Rodrigo. Can't remember their names."

"We'll reconnoiter," Zak said, and Vickers chuckled at the wry statement.

Calle Rodrigo was a short street wedged in between longer and wider ones, not far from the west edge of town. Beyond was the road north to Taos and south to Albuquerque. Zak caught a glimpse of it just before they turned the corner. Some of the adobes were two and three stories, and all looked sturdy and solid. The street had more shade than the others because of the taller buildings. In the middle of the street stood Biederman's Mercado, the mercantile store. Two doors down, with saddled horses tied to the hitchrings buried in the dirt, was La Copa Plata, with its English translation, "The Silver Cup," just below the sign on the false front. Both names were the same size. At the far end of the street, there were two hotels opposite each other, El Emporio and La Hacienda. Both looked equally seedy, and both posted equal prices for day, week, and month. $2.00 a night, $8.00 a week, $30.00 a month.

There was also a gun and saddle shop, an assay and land office, and a two-story house with flowers in pots on the porch, in planters hanging from the porch beams, and in beds.

"Biederman owns everything on this street, as far as I know," Vickers said.

"An ambitious man."

"Some say greedy, out at the fort."

"Maybe we can find out just what Mr. Biederman covets," Zak said as he pulled up at the hitchrail. He looked at all the brands on the horses, but didn't recognize any of them. Nor did Vickers.

"They're just horses to me," Jeff said. "Brands don't mean much in Santa Fe."

"Meaning?" Zak said.

Vickers laughed. "A running iron in this country is as common as a toothpick at Delmonico's in New York."

Zak dismounted, wrapped his reins around the hitchrail. He pulled his rifle from its boot and waited for Vickers. He and Jeff walked into the saloon and were met by a burly man wearing a linsey-woolsey shirt and denim pants, and with a hogleg strapped low on his right leg.

"Take your rifles, gents," the man said. "You won't need 'em in here. We got a gun case right over there. You can pick 'em up when you leave."

The talking stopped when the two men entered the saloon, rose up again as they strode to the bar without their rifles. Men sat at tables playing cards and dominoes, while others stood or sat at the long bar. There was a small stage and a slightly larger dance floor at one end of the long room. A Mexican with a guitar sat in a chair on the stage, but he was eating enchiladas and beans on a pewter plate. A bottle of soda pop sat on the floor next to the guitar, which was leaning on a large velvet cushion.

The bartender was a Mexican with high cheekbones and small, porcine eyes buried in the hollows behind them. He wore a bright bandanna around his neck and a shirt with the top buttons missing.

Zak and Jeff sat on stools at the end of the bar nearest the batwing doors. They put their boots on the rail, and Zak moved a spittoon aside to plant his other foot on the floor. The bartender moved toward them.

"*A su servicio,*" he said. "What is your pleasure, gentlemen?" He had a thick Mexican accent and a bright smile.

"*Dos cervezas,*" Zak said, holding up two fingers separated so that they formed a *V*.

"Are they cold?" Jeff asked.

"They are cool," the barkeep said.

The men at the other end of the bar pretended not to look at the two strangers, but it was plain to Zak that he and Jeff were being sized up by every one of them. And they did not look like merchants or ranchers, but hardcases. He turned and gazed idly at the men sitting at tables. He noticed there were two or three Mexican ladies sitting with some of the men, and one of them smiled at him. She had beautiful black hair, combed up in the back to form a graceful beehive, with ringlets dangling on both sides of her face, framing her startling beauty in a most becoming way. The barrettes in her hair sparkled with stones that might have been diamonds or cut glass. She wore a black velvet choker tight against her neck, and a pendant hung from it, just above her cleavage.

The bartender brought two earthen mugs of beer and set them in front of Jeff and Zak.

"If this is your first time at La Copa Plata, it is only five cents for the first beer," he said. "My name is Jorge Dominguez. *Bienvenidos a la Copa.*"

Zak looked at Jorge closely, then quickly took his gaze away. He wondered if Jorge was related to Renaldo Dominguez. Sergeant Dominguez. The traitor who had murdered Walsh and the other two soldiers. He wasn't going to ask. Not here. Not now. He glanced at Vickers to see if the name had made any impression on him. Apparently not, for Jeff was tasting the beer.

"It is a little cool," he said. "Not bad."

"They keep it in ollas. The clay sweats like a human and keeps the beer cool."

"You know more about it than I do. I haven't had a beer in two months, and the last one was hotter than a two-dollar pistol."

"Take it slow, Jeff. We want to keep our wits about us."

"I thought you'd be a whiskey man, Zak."

"Anything wet," Zak said with a wry smile.

"Well, if this is reconnoitering, it's better than a dusty ride out in the field."

"If anybody asks," Zak said, "we came in from Lordsburg. Ever been there?"

"Yes. Not much there."

"That's why we come from there. And before that, it's nobody's business."

"I understand," Jeff said.

One of the men, who had been watching them from behind another man at the far end of the bar, got up from his stool and walked toward them. He was carrying a whiskey glass in his hand.

"Buy you boys a drink?" the man said, leaning over the corner of the bar where it made its rounded turn.

"We're fine," Zak said.

"Just get in town?"

"Yes," Zak said.

The man looked at Vickers.

"He do all the talkin' for you, mister?"

"When he can get away with it," Vickers said, and the man smiled at the humor.

"Name's Pete Carmody," he said. "Where you boys from?"

"We rode in from Lordsburg, with a couple of stops in between," Zak said.

"Lordsburg, eh? Don't know a breathing soul there."

"Neither do we," Zak said. "It was just a place to throw down a bedroll, have a couple of whiskeys, and a plate of beans."

Pete beckoned to Dominguez, who came over and stood there.

"You give these boys anything they want, Jorge. It's on me."

"Thank you, Pete," Jeff said. Zak could have kicked him. He was almost too polite.

"Much obliged, Pete," Zak said.

"You lookin' for work, or just passin' through?" Pete said as Jorge walked to the other end of the bar, past all the bottles lined up against the large mirror and the painting of a half-naked lady.

"Maybe," Zak said. "We just about run out our string. Thought maybe we might find somethin' up Taos way."

"Taos, no. Nothin' but Injuns up thataway. Santa Fe's the place to be. There's opportunity here. You know which end to use of those rifles you brung in?"

"We've been known to bring down a rabbit or two," Zak said. "Sometimes a big old squirrel."

Pete laughed.

"You be here awhile, gents?"

"Awhile," Zak said. "Why?"

"I want to introduce you to Leo Biederman after the sun goes down. This place gets lively then, and he'll want to talk to you. If you're lookin' for honest work, that is."

"It doesn't have to be too honest," Zak said. "Or too much work."

Pete laughed again, and Zak knew he'd thrown out a line and the fish had taken the bait.

He lifted his glass in a salute to Pete Carmody, and Pete beamed.

Zak took a swig of beer and wiped foam from his mouth. So far, so good, he thought, and they hadn't even finished with the introductions yet.

Carmody had more questions for his newfound friends. He tipped his hat back in a friendly gesture, put a leg up on the brass rail. His hair was a mop of rust-red yarn that skewed in all directions as if it had escaped from a weaver's loom.

"Where'bouts in town you stayin'?" he asked Vickers.

"No place, yet."

"We saw a couple of hotels down the block," Zak said. "Thought we'd wet our whistles first then mosey on down the street and see where we can put up our horses and get a clean bed."

Carmody raised his hand and gestured to Jorge, who quickstepped his way back down to the end of the bar.

"Jorge, dig out a couple of chits for my friends here. The Hacienda ought to suit 'em."

"Yes, sir, Mr. Carmody."

"I don't believe you told me your names," Carmody said. "I know it ain't real polite to ask, but if we're going to do business together . . ."

"I'm Jeff Vickers."

"Zak Cody."

Carmody shook hands with both men. Dominguez returned with two slips of paper. He handed them to Carmody, along with a pencil stub. Carmody wrote something on each slip and initialed it. Then he handed the chits to Vickers, who was sitting nearest to him.

"You just give these to the desk clerk at the Hacienda, Jeff. Rooms are clean. Good beds."

"Thanks, Pete," Zak said as Jeff slipped the chits into his shirt pocket.

"There's a stable behind the hotel. When you're ready to mosey on down there, I'll send someone to show you where you can board your horses."

"We're just going to have this one beer, Pete," Zak said. "We're plumb tuckered. We'll get our rooms and be back tonight to meet Mr. Biederman."

"That's just fine. Hold on."

Carmody spoke to Dominguez. "Tell Ralph to come on down here, will you, Jorge?"

Jorge nodded and walked to the other end of the bar. He leaned over the bar and whispered to one of the men seated there. He cocked a thumb in Carmody's direction. A moment later a shorter man walked over to join Carmody. He had a square jaw, thick neck, Teutonic features, pale, lifeless blue eyes.

"This here's Ralph Zigler," Carmody said. "Ralph, shake hands with Jeff Vickers and Zak Cody."

Zigler offered a chubby hand to both Zak and Jeff. He squeezed the blood out of both hands, but his face never changed expression.

Zak looked him over without making a point of it. It took only a glance to see that Zigler knew how to carry himself. He had straight hair the color of barn straw that spiked downward from under his hat. There was a scar on the bridge of his nose and another under one cheek.

"It is good to meet you," Ralph said in a thick Germanic accent. "I buy you a beer, eh?"

"No, Ralph," Carmody said. "I want you to take them down to the Hacienda when they're ready and show them where the stables are."

"That is good," Ralph said. "I will do that."

The man had no expression on his face. He spoke as if he were reading a document or reciting from memory. Perhaps he was. English was not his native language.

The pretty Mexican woman stood up from her table and caught Zak's eye. She unfolded a small colored fan in front of her face. Her eyes danced with light. She let the fan drop and flashed Zak a warm smile. He nodded to her. He knew the language of the Spanish fan, a little, and knew the woman was flirting with him. She sat back down and continued her conversation with the men at her table.

Zak wondered if all the men in the saloon worked for Biederman. There was no way to tell, but none had the look of ranchers or farmers, whose faces often reflected the serenity of the land they worked, or their feel for cattle, sheep, and horses. These men looked like road agents, with their sullen, half-lidded, shifty eyes and drawn features. He didn't sense friendliness from any of those who glanced his way.

As for Pete Carmody, he sounded like an organized man, a leader, just the kind of man who could mount a campaign against men like Gregorio Delacruz and put the fear of death square in their hearts.

Ralph Zigler was more difficult to read. He gave no sign of what he was thinking or how he felt. He was as cold as a chunk of pig iron, and those flat, blue-gray eyes of his were icier than a frozen river, a pane of glass covered with snow. Zigler could see out, but nobody could see in; that was the impression that Zak got from looking at him. He had seen men like Zigler before. He had seen Lakota braves and Pawnee scouts, Crow and Blackfoot warriors with that same empty look, the look of a stone killer, as merciless as wind and rain, or fire.

Zak and Jeff finished their beers, shoved their mugs away, got up from their stools.

"Thanks for the beer, Pete," Zak said.

"Ralph here will take care of you. See you both tonight."

"Right," Zak said.

Zak glanced at the Mexican woman as he and Jeff followed Zigler to the batwing doors. She spoke with her fan again, striking an alluring pose behind its pleated flare. It was almost a curtsy, the way she did it—and she was sitting down.

The man who had taken their rifles came up to them and handed their weapons back. He smiled for the first time, flashing gold teeth.

"Come back real soon," he said in a drawl Zak could not immediately identify. Southern. Georgia or Mississippi, he thought.

They walked to the hitchrail.

"You can ride your horses down to the Haci-enda, or with me you can walk," Zigler said in his mangled English.

Jeff looked at Zak as he was preparing to mount.

"We'll walk with you, Ralph," Zak said. "Might get some of the kinks out my legs."

"Yes, it is good to walk after a long ride. Did you come far?"

"Lordsburg," Jeff said, as if to show Zak that he remembered the lie.

"Yes, that is far," Zigler said.

They passed the false front on an adobe with windows. The sign read LA FRONTERA LAND OF-FICE. Beneath the store name was the subtitle L & M ENTERPRISES. Next to that was L & M MINING COMPANY, with its notice: ASSAYS, CLAIMS, GOLD & SILVER BOUGHT AND SOLD. Many of the other businesses had the same name out front, such as the L & M Patent Office and the L & M Outfitters & Guide Service, with hunting, fishing, trophies, and taxidermy listed beneath its name.

Zigler waved at people who were standing in the doorways of those businesses, or who were looking through the glass windows out onto the street. Zak said nothing, but his mind was stak-ing out ideas in a grid that he hoped he would be able to connect with strings of information. There were customers—horses tied in front, small carts and wagons—at nearly every business. The street seemed to be thriving. To Zak, it felt like a minia-ture city within a city, almost like in the financial district of New York, where stocks and bonds were traded on a daily basis, generating thousands of dollars for bankers, stockbrokers, and wealthy clients. Zigler offered no explanation for any of the businesses.

"Here's the hotel," Zigler said. "Out in the back is the stables. I will take you there?"

"Sure," Zak said. "We've got to stay at the Hacienda. Might as well get our horses boarded and grained."

"They will do that," the laconic Ralph said.

Zak was not surprised that the painted sign on the stables read L & M LIVERY STABLES. Beneath it, more information: BOARDING, FEED, LIVESTOCK BOUGHT AND SOLD.

The stableman, Dagoberto Elizando, was a man in his fifties with a face sculpted out of bronze. He was wearing a straw sombrero and gloves, and boots that had seen better days. Zigler spoke to him out of Zak and Jeff's earshot, and Zak saw Elizando nodding and grinning as he glanced at the strangers.

There were horses in the stalls, some out in a corral in back of the large wood-and-adobe barn. Zak smelled the heady scents of hay, corn, wheat, and manure, threaded with horse sweat and urine.

"You do not have to pay," Zigler said cryptically as he led Zak and Jeff to a back entrance of the hotel.

"Why not?" Zak asked.

"Of the hotel, you are guests," Zigler said.

They got two rooms and said good-bye to Zigler at the front desk.

"To the Silver Cup, you will come later, no?"

"Yes," Zak said. "Sometime after sunset."

"Good," Zigler said and marched through the lobby, with its flowers, small trees, and cactus plants in colorful clay pots that had been painted and glazed so that their surfaces were shiny, almost like porcelain.

The clerk took their chits and turned the ledger toward them, handing Vickers a pen. He was an older man who wore spectacles and garters on his sleeves, a green eyeshade, brushy moustache, fuzzy gray sideburns. He had delicate, veined hands and a face frozen in a permanent scowl, as if afflicted with rheumatism that pained every joint in his body.

He handed them two keys.

"My name's Cletus Fargo. I'm the day clerk. Slim Gardner comes on at night. No shootin' up the rooms, no settin' the beddin' on fire. Chamber pot's on the bureau, slop jar's under the bed, but you got an outhouse at the side of the buildin' nearest the Taos road. Numbers Four and Five, gents. Make yourselves to home."

With that, Fargo turned and went into a little office and sat down. He closed his eyes, leaned back in an overstuffed chair, and put his feet up on a desk or table.

Zak threw his saddlebags on the bed, laid his rifle next to them while Vickers opened the door to Number Five.

"Jeff, come on over once you get settled," Zak said, having left his door open. He slipped his key in his pocket and sat in a chair. There was a window that gave him a view of the Taos road and the Sangre de Cristo range, with its snowcapped peaks shining alabaster white in the sun.

When Jeff came in, devoid of his saddlebags and

rifle, Zak told him to close the door and waved him to a chair. There were two chairs in the room, a small table, a chest of drawers, and pegs on the wall that served as a wardrobe. There were painted pictures of desert flowers and a golden eagle on two of the walls.

"Looks like we passed muster," Jeff said. "At least with Pete Carmody."

"He sure is spooning honey on our biscuits," Zak said.

"What do you make of Zigler?"

"Don't turn your back on either one of them," Zak said.

"So, now what? We going to the Silver Cup tonight?"

"I'm curious about Leo Biederman. I got the impression that he's recruiting men—gunmen—for something. And I've got an idea what he's after."

"You do?"

"I'll keep it to myself for now, Jeff. I just wanted to give you a warning."

"A warning?"

"Ever been to San Francisco or Monterey?"

Vickers shook his head.

"When a ship docks, say from China or Japan or India, sometimes the sailors jump ship in port. When that captain has to sail again, he gets his crew from the saloons along the waterfront. Old Chinese practice."

"I didn't know that."

"They put knockout drops in a man's whiskey, or club him with belaying pins in an alley if he's had a snootful. And then they carry these poor jaspers onboard ship just before they sail. When the poor bastards wake up, they're far out at sea and won't see land again for many months. They call this practice 'shanghai.' When they shanghai you, you're virtually a prisoner of the captain and the vessel."

"Why are you telling me this, Zak?"

"If you drink whiskey tonight, don't swallow a mouthful with the first swig. Let the whiskey trickle past your lips. If your lips tingle a little or you feel like you have a thistle in your mouth, don't drink any more. Just pretend, and pour the whiskey into your boot."

"You think they might try to shanghai us?" Jeff said.

"I mean, keep your wits about you. Let me do most of the talking. You do all the listening."

"Aye, aye, sir," Vickers joked.

"Ever been to Shanghai, Jeff? Me, neither. And let's not go there tonight."

Two hours later Zak tapped on Jeff's door. He had napped and watched the traffic on the Taos road as the sun went down over the mountains. After it turned dark, the road emptied and there was a quiet on the land outside his window.

Like the quiet before a storm.

⇌ 16 ⇌

Zak and Jeff left their keys at the front desk and walked outside the hotel. The street was nearly deserted except in front of La Copa Plata, which was lined with horses and men standing outside, their cigarettes glowing in the dusk, their voices floating down the adobe canyon lined with closed shops.

"Nice evening," Jeff said. "I wonder what's going on at the post."

"Put those matters out of your mind, Jeff. We have more important things to do."

"I'm trying my best to be unmilitary."

Zak laughed. "It's probably something you can't do. You can wear civilian clothes, but there's starch in your backbone and that doesn't wash out easily."

"Does it show?"

"If anybody asks why you stand so straight, tell them you got bucked off your horse."

"So, I look stiff," Jeff said.

"As an iron flagpole," Zak said, then stepped onto the street. Light from the hotel threw a parallelogram in front, and an oil lamp near the entrance made their shadows loom long across the dirt street, spilled its own light into a warped circular pool that wavered with the flicker of the flame inside the glass.

Zak stopped, put out a hand to hold Vickers back. Across the street, in the shadows, he saw the glow of a cigarette. His hand dropped to the butt of his pistol. Jeff saw the orange glow, too, and slid his hand down his hip until he felt the grip of his sidearm.

"Zak," a voice called.

"Show yourself," Zak said, easing his pistol an inch out of his holster.

"It's me, Randy Bullard. Maybe you better walk over here, out of the light."

Zak let the pistol fall back snug into his holster. Jeff breathed a sigh and relaxed his own gun hand.

"What in hell are you doing here, Sergeant?" Vickers demanded. "And how did you know where to find us?"

"Sir, I come down to Biederman's to buy some store-boughts. Since Colonel Loomis is planning a campaign, I thought this would be my last chance. I got a pass."

"And you knew where to find us?" Zak said.

"I had a drink at the Silver Cup with some of the other troopers who come in with me. I got to get back, but I heard tell about two new hardcases in town what was stayin' at the Hacienda. I figgered it was you two."

"Randy," Zak said, "does Naldo Dominguez have a brother?"

Bullard dropped the butt of his cigarette on the street, ground it out with his heel.

"Yeah, he sure does. Forgot about that. Jorge. He works at the Silver Cup."

"Did you see him when you had your drink?" Zak asked.

"Nope. He only works days, I think."

"Is this what you came down here to tell us, Sergeant?" Vickers said. "We know about the campaign and Colonel Loomis."

"No, sir, I come to tell Zak here, I mean the colonel, that a while ago, that sheeper rancher, Delacruz, he come to the Presidio. They sent him over to see Colonel Loomis."

Zak felt his breath hold fast in his lungs. Bullard had caught him by surprise.

"Do you know what Gregorio told the colonel?" Zak asked.

"Hell, two privates, a corporal, and a sergeant-at-arms heard him tell Colonel Loomis that his neighbor had eighty, ninety head of sheep run off last night by Navajos. He said it was Narbona and Largos. His neighbor, a feller by the name of Lorenzo Villareal, got told by Narbona the same thing he told old Delacruz. Go tell the soldiers to come."

"Any white men with Narbona?"

"Delacruz said no."

"Why didn't Villareal come in with Gregorio?" Zak asked.

"The way Delacruz told it, he was buryin' some herders. His wife and daughter got stole, too. Delacruz is plumb scairt out of his wits."

"Where is Delacruz now, Randy? Do you know?"

"He didn't go back to his ranch, that's for sure. I think he knows people here in Santa Fe. He was asking for military protection, same as Villareal. There's somethin' else you maybe ought to know."

"What's that, Sergeant?" Vickers said.

"Colonel Loomis ain't goin' to wait no three days to go after Narbona. He's hoppin' mad and issued orders to his officers to be ready to ride out tomorrow."

"Tomorrow?" Zak said.

"Yes, sir, that's why I got to get back. I just come in to get some Piedmonts. Each man is to carry a week's rations, fifty rounds of rifle ammunition, slickers, and tents."

"Anything else, Randy?" Zak asked.

"Yeah, he's takin' artillery with him, mountain howitzers, a couple of four-pounders, maybe a Gatling gun."

"Shit," Vickers said. "Zak, I have to go back to Fort Marcy."

"You're staying with me, Jeff."

"But—"

"No argument. Randy, you haven't seen us. Now, get on back to the post. Thanks for the information."

"You be careful, Zak. You, too, Captain Vickers."

"Don't you salute us, Randy," Zak said. "Somebody might be watching."

Zak and Jeff walked away, leaving Bullard in the shadows. Vickers seemed ready to explode, but he held his tongue.

"Loomis double-crossed us," he whispered to Zak when they were well away from Bullard.

"I figured he couldn't wait three days," Zak said.

"You did?"

"That's why we've got to finish our business tonight."

"Tonight?"

"If we can. I have a hunch we'll know more by morning than we do now."

"How's that?" Vickers asked.

"If you can't beat 'em," Zak said, "join up with 'em."

"Yes, but we've got loyalties and duties and—"

"And we'll stay loyal and do our duties, Jeff. Now, go back to being a civilian. We're almost there."

La Copa Plata was a blazing beacon of light in the darkness of the street. The strains of lively music, guitars, trumpet, drums, blared out into night, and the sound of voices was a low drone under the melody.

As soon as Jeff and Zak cleared the batwing doors, Pete Carmody strode up to greet them, a grin on his face as wide and white as a bib.

"Leo's right over there, gents," he said with a wide sweep of his arm. "Just follow me."

Zak spotted the man in the center of the room. He looked like a king holding court. He was a tall, broad-shouldered man with a ruddy face, wearing a white Stetson. He looked like a Washington politician, except for the hat, which would have put him squarely in Texas. But all the other attributes were there: the ready smile; the hearty handshake; the wet, puckered lips, suitable for kissing babies and young mothers.

"Mr. Biederman—Leo—this is Zak Cody and Jeff Vickers, the two men I told you about."

The woman sitting next to Biederman had a face that appeared carved out of dark teak, with high cheekbones; a small, pudgy nose; bright brown eyes; and hair so black it shone like a crow's wing under the spray of the lamplight. She had rouge on her cheeks and lipstick the color of blood on her thin mouth. Her clothes were fancy—black lace with trims of red and green woven into the sleeves and collar.

"I'm Leo, and this is my wife, Minnie," he said, gesturing to the woman. "Minnie's a full-blood Navajo lady and the light of my life."

Minnie didn't smile but looked at Zak darkly, skimmed her glance over Jeff, and then shifted back to Zak, appraising him with hooded eyes.

After the "pleasedtameetchas" Leo told Jeff and Zak to sit down, then raised a hand in the air. The band stopped playing "Green Grow the Lilacs," paused, and then broke into *La Macarena*," the song that was always played at bullfights in Spain and Mexico.

Zak sensed that they were sitting with a shrewd man who played his cards close to his vest. Behind the twinkle in Leo's merry eyes, there were shadows that disguised his true feelings. He exuded power, like magnetized steel, whether he was standing or sitting—it emanated from him. He watched Vickers, who seemed awestruck by the magnanimous gestures and flamboyant manner of Leo Biederman. But Zak kept his eyes on Minnie, who had her own quiet strength. He could see the tears of her people in the lines etched into her face, feel the great sorrow and pride of an entire race who had once owned land that stretched farther than the eye could see. She, too, was magnetic, but in a different way from her husband. She was the rock and granite of the mountain, while he was the ermine snow shining on its peak, supported by a woman who had once walked with giants of her own race and now found herself surrounded by fawning, obsequious lackeys who thought the world owed them a living. She, Zak could see, felt that it was the other way around. Her people owned the earth and nurtured it, roamed it, hunted on it, but never staked a claim to either water or dirt.

"Tell me, Cody," Leo was saying, "what brought you out West to our part of this great country?"

Leo's laughing expression had vanished from his eyes, and he wore a serious and skeptical frown.

"Possibilities," Zak said.

Leo's face went blank for a second; then he reared back in his chair and roared like a bull. "Haw, that's what you got here, son! Possibilities. Ain't no end to 'em. And about you, Mr. Vickers, do you share that dream?"

"I go Zak one more, Mr. Biederman," Jeff said. "Probabilities. *Carpe diem*. That's my motto."

"Ah, you are a scholar, I see. Latin. Yes, that's my motto, as well. 'Seize the day.' Make hay while the sun shines, gather ye rosebuds while ye may."

"You've got us tagged, Leo," Zak said. "We shucked off civilization and all its trappings, came to the heart of the trading world, Santa Fe, the center of the universe."

"You're a man after my own heart, Cody," Leo said. "Now, Pete tells me you're looking for honest work."

"Did he say 'honest'? I don't think that word was ever spoken by me."

"It's a figure of speech, of course. Work is its own reward, of course."

"Of course," Zak said.

Jeff licked his lips, and a waiter appeared to take their orders. The Mexican band played a mournful tune from Jalisco, a sad song of love and betrayal and a woman's tears at the foot of the gallows tree where her man swings in the wind, his neck broken by a thick rope knotted just under his ear.

"Whiskey," Vickers said.

"I'll have the same," Zak said and saw Leo nod his approval.

He noticed that Pete was not drinking and there was no sign of the German, Zigler.

"Do you know anything about our history, Cody?"

"Some. Not much."

"First were the Navajos, of course. Then, the Spaniards—damn their black hides—came, and then the Mexicans revolted, the poor people and the Indios swept the bastards out of Taos and cut their balls off in Santa Fe. And then the Santa Fe Trail opened up our city to the east and to the world. And the gringos took the country at the point of a gun and subjugated the Mexicans just like the Mexicans conquered the Indios. One bloody battle after another, with Kearney and Carson and Washington. Now we got soldiers running the damned government, and all the Navajos tucked away on god-awful reservations, where they can't grow corn or beans or anything but dog shit and disease."

"Pretty grim history, all right," Zak said.

Leo turned his hand into a fist and slammed it into the table. The glasses shook and some of the men at the surrounding tables jumped in surprise, drawing back in their chairs.

"The army don't know what land is, what riches can be got from it. All they do is build forts and dams and strut around looking like peacocks, when all they are is banty roosters. We don't need an army here. We ain't prisoners."

"You're right about that, Leo," Vickers said, and Zak was proud of him at that moment. "Anywhere the damned army is, you got people with jackboots on their necks."

Zak tried not to show his surprise.

"Gentlemen," Leo said, leaning over the table in a conspiratorial manner, "maybe you'd like to be part of a great enterprise. Join me and you'll see the army tuck its tail and run all the way back to the east where they belong, and the lands open up again, prosperity and freedom return to a great country where the races mingle and thrive, and riches flow like the milk and honey of a new Canaan."

The waiter appeared with their drinks and Leo leaned back in his chair as if he had just finished revealing a great secret.

The band struck up a lively mariachi and men danced with pretty women and laughter rippled through the room.

Zak took a swallow of whiskey and felt its fortifying heat. He looked at Leo hard and long.

He was certain, now, that the man who sat across from him at the table was mad—truly mad.

But for the first time that evening, he saw the flicker of a smile on Minnie's face.

Though insane and megalomaniacal, Leo was a hero, plain to see, in her eyes.

And perhaps, Zak thought, the savior of her people.

⊰ 17 ⊱

Before he had finished his whiskey, Zak realized that Leo was waiting for someone. He kept looking toward the batwing doors and over at Pete, who also held a fascination for those swinging, slatted pieces of wood.

So far, Leo had not divulged his "divine plan," but Zak sensed that he was ready to sweep him and Jeff up into his camp and make them both true believers in his cause.

Leo smoked cigars and the table was wreathed in blue smoke. Minnie smoked a cheroot, held it as daintily as any court maid back in England. She did not drink whiskey, though. She drank tea, not from a cup, but from a glass, so that anyone would think she was right up there with the boys, swigging down hard liquor with the best of them.

Beneath the raucous music, Zak heard the *whick-snick* of cards being dealt, the clatter of wooden poker chips, the clanking of bottles and jars, and the reedy thrum of masculine voices intermingled with the high, lyrical curl of women's laughter. As he sat there, he longed for the quiet of a lonesome hill, a solitary camp by a woodland creek or the peace that came when a man lay on the prairie at night and stared up at billions of diamonds. He was not a man for saloons and city lights, but someone who felt at home in the wild. He drew comfort from the simple sight of a deer grazing in a meadow, a gold aspen leaf jiggling in the wind, sunlight dappling the freckled backs of brook trout in a clear stream, the towering mountains when the shade under their brow was deep lavender.

Zak noticed that waiters were carrying trays of food to some of the tables. His stomach roiled with hunger. "Mr. Biederman, Leo, Jeff and I haven't taken supper yet. Will you excuse us? We'll get another table and order."

"By all means. And supper's on me, Cody. You and Jeff eat hearty, then join us later for some fine brandy."

Jeff scooted his chair back from the table. He bowed to Minnie, and Zak nodded to her as he left the Biederman party. Pete smiled at them.

Zak chose a table along the wall that seemed more isolated from the throng. He and Jeff sat down. A waiter brought them slates with the evening's fare written in chalk. They both ordered *bistecas y papas*.

"Mr. Biederman has requested me to serve you wine with your supper," the waiter said. "Would you prefer a French burgundy, or perhaps a sauterne?"

"Burgundy," Zak said before Jeff could say anything.

"Perfect," Jeff said, and they grinned at each other.

The waiter left and Zak leaned over the table, a look of earnestness on his face, his eyes narrowed, his gaze intense.

"Jeff," he said, "why did you join the army, go to VMI?"

"What an odd question, Zak."

"Can you answer it?"

"Sure. My daddy was in the army, and so was my grandpa. I grew up on an army post. My father was a sergeant major when he was killed at Harper's Ferry. I suppose I wanted revenge. But it was also a way to escape my mother."

"That's an honest answer, anyway."

"My mother made life at home a living hell. Which was why my father preferred the field of battle. There, he had a chance of winning."

"Are you loyal to the army?"

"Of course. Why do you ask?"

"Leo Biederman has a different opinion. You seemed willing to back him up."

"I'm an actor tonight. You said so. I was playing my part."

"That's good."

"How about you, Zak? You're still in the army, even though you don't have to join muster, salute, or obey orders."

"The army gave to me. I'm giving some of it back."

"What did the army ever do for you?" Jeff asked.

"It gave me an education, gave me good friends, made me into some kind of man, good or bad."

"That's an honest answer, too, I guess. But, you're not even army material, at least by my standards."

"And what are your standards, Jeff?"

"VMI standards, I guess. You don't look army, you don't act army, yet you enjoy the friendship of fighting men like General Crook and General—now President—Grant. You're a rare breed. But you don't really fit in. At least you don't fit in anywhere I've been or anyplace I know."

"Does whiskey loosen your tongue like that, Jeff?" Vickers smiled.

"I suppose so. It just came out. I've been studying you, Zak, ever since I saw you up on the flat when I got back from Delacruz's sheep ranch. I guess I'm getting an inkling of why people call you the Shadow Rider. You are outside the circle of most any group. You just don't fit, and that bothers any military man—bothers me. We are used to discipline and duty, taking and giving orders, never questioning, but taking 'arms against a sea of troubles' on this earth, 'and by opposing end them.'"

"So, you are a scholar, as Biederman said. Shakespeare falls trippingly off your tongue."

Vickers smiled.

"You have evidently read a book or two yourself, Zak."

The steaks arrived on warm pewter plates. The waiter brought flatware wrapped in napkins, a bottle of burgundy, and two wineglasses.

Both men avoided looking over at Leo's table until they were finished eating.

"Good wine," Jeff said.

"The steak was as tough as an army boot," Zak said.

"You've eaten an army boot?"

"And a belt or two," Zak said.

The two got up from their table and walked over to Biederman's group. Pete waved a hand at their empty chairs.

"Saved them for you," he said.

Biederman pulled two cigars out of his vest pocket, handed them across the table. Jeff took one. Zak waved the other one away.

"Don't smoke," he said.

Biederman's eyebrows arched as he drew back his head and stared at Zak in disbelief.

He put the other cigar back in his pocket.

"How about some brandy, then?" Leo said.

"Sure," Zak said.

"Good. I own a vineyard and this is *Aguardiente*, made with my own grapes. Someday, maybe I'll show you my winery. It's up in Taos, but I may open one here. Soon, maybe."

Zak's ear was attuned to the nuances of Leo's speech, and his last two words sparked his interest. Biederman was a man with plans, and it was evident that he intended to expand his business interests.

So far, though, Leo had not divulged any secrets, not expressed his intentions. But Zak was almost certain that Biederman intended building an empire around and in Santa Fe, and that he resented the army's intrusion into his affairs. It was a good bet that Leo had something to do with the recent raids along the Rio Grande. He could not prove it, but there was strong evidence that Biederman was behind the Navajo uprisings, because Pete and Ralph had been with Narbona when they struck the Delacruz ranch. He was only surprised that the two men had been so open about it, not concealing their faces.

Biederman, Zak decided, seemed pretty sure of himself. He might be in the background, but his men were pretty brash and bold. Why? Didn't Biederman care? What was he planning, exactly? Did he want to lure the army into Navajo lands in the Jemez and once they were there, come out in the open with his scheme? If so, it was a pretty bold move, even for a man with Leo's confidence. Perhaps he had an ace in the hole that Zak didn't know about.

Perhaps he had more than one ace up his sleeve.

Leo snapped his fingers and a waiter appeared with a tray, two bottles of L & M *Aguardiente*, and a half dozen snifters. The waiter set the glasses around, one before Leo, another in front of Minnie, one each for Pete, Jeff, and Zak, and the last one at an empty place.

"Tell Clarita to join us, Fred, will you?" Biederman said to the waiter.

"Yes, sir."

Fred uncorked one bottle, poured brandy in each snifter, except for the one at the empty place. He set the bottle down, left, and a few seconds later the woman with the fan came to the table. Pete got up and pulled her chair out. The chair was next to Zak's place at the table.

"Clarita, this is Mr. Zak Cody, and his friend is Mr. Jeff Vickers. Cody, this is Miss Clarita Mendez. Fred pour some brandy for Clarita, will you?"

"Of course," Fred replied and poured brandy into her glass.

She set her fan on the table and raised her glass to her nose. She sniffed it and nodded to Leo.

"This is your best yet, Leo," she said.

"Why, thank you, my dear," he said.

"Cody, Miss Mendez is the daughter of a prominent Santa Fe judge. She expressed an interest in meeting you. So, let's drink to that meeting."

"I'm flattered," Clarita said. She had only a slight accent.

Zak said nothing, but lifted his glass to her, then drank some of the brandy. It warmed his mouth and throat, then hit his stomach like a fireball. The fumes from the snifter made him slightly dizzy for a few seconds. His eyes watered and he gulped in air.

"Very fine brandy," Zak said, and Leo laughed, upended his own glass, and drained the snifter without a trace of discomfort.

Clarita put her hands in her lap and one of them brushed against Zak's leg. He did not move his leg, but something inside him twisted a turn or two, as if an auger had bitten into his flesh.

Jeff coughed as the fumes struck his nostrils and the brandy scorched his tongue.

Leo didn't bat an eye.

"You two have been drinking too much cheap red-eye," he said. "Brandy is good for the soul, isn't that right, Minnie?"

"You are right, my husband," Minnie said, but she hadn't touched her drink.

Leo's gaze shifted to the doorway again and this time, his eyes widened. Zak turned slightly and saw, out of the corner of his eye, two men enter the cantina.

One of them was Jorge Dominguez.

The other was Ralph Zigler.

They made straight for Leo's table. Jorge hung back, but Ralph leaned over and whispered something to Leo. Jorge looked at Clarita and nodded. A look passed between them.

"All right, Ralph. You and Jorge get something to eat. I'll talk to you both later."

The two men walked toward the bar. Leo struck a match, bit off the end of a fresh cigar, and lit it. He stretched his hand across the table toward Jeff. Jeff bit off the end of his cigar, leaned into the light, and puffed on his cigar.

Smoke shrouded the glasses, bottles, and tabletop.

"Cody, do you and Vickers wish to join my gallant band of mercenaries? The pay is one hundred dollars a month and found, but I promise you riches beyond your dreams, once we have accomplished our mission."

"Just what is your mission, Leo?" Zak asked, and he felt Clarita's hand squeeze his knee under the table.

"Let's just say you'll be acting as messengers. Pete and Ralph will show you what to do. Tomorrow, before dawn, you'll slip out of town and cross the Rio Grande. There will be some other men going with you."

Leo pulled out a wad of greenbacks, peeled off two hundred-dollar bills. He handed one to Zak, the other to Jeff.

"Here's your first month's pay, but there will be a bonus if you're successful, payable upon your return."

"Messengers?" Jeff said.

"And observers, shall we say? Easy work, but lots of riding in rough country."

"Where is this rough country?" Zak asked.

Leo smiled.

"Ever been to the Jemez?" he said.

Both Jeff and Zak shook their heads.

"Ever hear of it?"

Again, both men indicated they had not.

"You'll see it tomorrow. Now you'd better get a good night's sleep. Pete will wake you when it's time to saddle up. He'll have grub and water for you and extra ammunition."

"It sounds to me like you're planning to start a war," Zak said. He made it sound offhand, as a joking statement, but he was dead serious.

"Ah, you never know, Cody. Wars start over women, water rights, land, and politics. Some say the war between the whites and the Navajos never ended."

"So?" Zak said, pressing for an answer.

Leo blew a cloud of smoke into the air. Gone was his affability, his charm, gone in that one puff of his cigar and the blown smoke.

"So, maybe someone is going to hold up a flag of truce, Cody. Maybe the war will finally be over."

"And the winner . . . ?" Zak said, his eyes narrowed to slits.

Leo shrugged.

"Who knows?" he said. "War is unpredictable. So is peace. But, to the victor belong the spoils. And when the stakes are very high, the spoils can be something grand."

"Do I have to kill anybody?" Zak said with a look of innocence on his face.

"Do you want to kill somebody, Cody?" Leo asked.

"Not right now," Zak said, and everyone at the table laughed except Minnie.

Clarita found Zak's hand under the table and pressed something into it. Then she closed up his fingers. It felt like a piece of paper rolled up tight. He slipped the paper into his pocket and stood up.

"Good night, then," Zak said. Then to Pete, "See you in the morning."

"Sleep tight," Pete said.

Zak and Jeff walked outside and headed for the hotel. Neither spoke until they were well away from the Silver Cup.

"Are you going to ride with Pete in the morning?" Jeff asked.

"What do you think, Jeff?" Zak said, and the lamplight cast his face into a saffron mask with hard shadows along the jawline.

Somewhere a dog barked and they heard the chords of a guitar coming from the saloon. The moon hung in the sky like a great eye dripping quicksilver onto the adobe walls and dirt streets, as shadows skulked around them like a pack of prowling wolves.

⊸ 18 ⊸

Zak grabbed Jeff's arm and led him between two buildings before they reached the hotel.

Jeff jerked his arm away.

"What in hell are you doing?" he said.

"Just follow me, Jeff. You made a good target out there on the street."

"What in hell are you talking about, Zak?"

"I only caught a couple of words, but that was enough to tell me that you're in danger. Maybe both of us are."

Zak went through the passageway and headed toward the livery stables. Jeff matched his gait, stride for stride.

"Do you mind telling me just what the hell you're talking about, Zak? I don't like to be kept in the dark."

"Right now, Jeff, that's the safest place for you."

"You're not making any sense," Vickers said.

"Well, when Zigler spoke to Biederman in the saloon, he spoke in German. He was whispering but I caught a couple of words, *soldaten* and *kapitän*. He didn't mention your name, or at least I didn't hear it, but Zigler was talking about you."

"What do those words mean?"

"Soldier and captain. Zigler knows you're in the army. And the way Dominguez was looking at you, I knew the cat was out of the bag. Biederman couldn't wait for us to get out of that saloon."

"He wants us to go on a mission with Pete tomorrow."

"I expect the only mission Leo wants us to go on is into the hereafter."

"Are you sure, Zak? I missed all that."

They reached the stables. Zak drew his pistol and reached out an arm to press Vickers up against the adobe wall out front. He held a hand to his lips. They both stood there, listening.

Then Zak entered the barn.

"Saddle your horse, Jeff. Quick. Then we'll get our rifles and saddlebags out of the room. But we want to be ready to ride."

"Where are we going?"

"First, to Fort Marcy. I can't let Loomis take those troops into the field tomorrow. I think he'll be marching right into a trap."

They saddled their horses and then went inside the hotel, leaving the horses rein-tied just inside the barn. Zak went to the front desk, which was empty, and retrieved their keys from the mail slots. The two men entered their rooms in the dark, picked up their rifles, saddlebags, and bedrolls, then, leaving their keys inside the rooms, they returned to the livery stables.

As they mounted their horses, Zak felt the rolled up paper in his pocket and remembered that Clarita had slipped it into his hand.

"Got a match, Jeff?" he asked.

Jeff struck a match as Zak unrolled the piece of paper. There was writing on it.

"It's in Spanish," Jeff said. "You understand the lingo?"

The note read, "*Cuidado con Jorge Dominguez. Es un matador. Quiere matarte esta noche.*" There was more, but the rest of it dealt with a past, a past he had thought he'd forgotten—a past he had tried to put behind him, where it belonged.

"Clarita gave me this note in the cantina. It tells me to watch out for Jorge Dominguez. 'He's a killer,' she says, and is out to kill me. Tonight."

"Do you trust her?"

"I don't know. But a warning is a warning. I trust that. Jorge's brother is a traitor. Maybe it runs in the family."

The match went out, and the two men sat there, listening to what sounded like furtive footsteps. The sound seemed to come from alongside the hotel.

Jeff cleared his throat.

"Shouldn't we be going, Zak? If Jorge is—"

"Shhh," Zak said, and held the bit tight against the back of Nox's mouth.

The sound vanished.

"There was more to the note," Zak said. He remembered what Clarita had written. "*Recuerdas mi padre, Paquito? Recuerdas mi hermana, Corazon?*"

"Yeah? What else?" Jeff whispered.

"She asked me if I remembered her father, Paquito. And she asked me if I remembered her sister, Corazon."

"Did you know this woman, this Clarita, before?"

"I had forgotten," Zak said.

"She's a beautiful woman. Hard to forget."

She wasn't a woman then. She was a little girl. A little girl in pigtails."

"Zak, what about her sister? What was her name . . . Corazon?"

"Yes," Zak said. "I remember her sister." He paused, let out a sigh. "I wondered what happened to her."

"To Clarita?"

"No, she was just a little girl. Maybe nine or ten. Cute little thing."

"You're holding something back on me, Zak."

"Jeff, my father died in Taos. He was murdered there by a man named Ben Trask. I hunted Trask down and turned him over to the Apache chief, Cochise, who staked him out on an anthill and watched him die, real slow. What they call an Apache Sundown. Trask brutally murdered my father, stole his gold, and . . ."

"And you got both justice and revenge."

"Yes. Corazon was my father's true love. He was going to marry her."

"What was your father's name? Paquito?"

"No, my father's name was Russell Cody. Paquito was Corazon's father. He's Clarita's father."

"And . . . you know him?"

"Leo said her father was a judge, but he didn't tell me her father's first name, which was Francisco. But everyone called him Paquito."

"Man, you have a history here in New Mexico, don't you?"

"I guess I do," Zak said.

Zak held up his hand. A sliver of moonlight slashed across it like a mercurial scar.

There was a rustling of cloth, something scraping against the adobe wall of the hotel or the building next to it. Then the crunch of a foot on gravel.

"I hear it," Jeff whispered.

Both men drew their pistols, but did not cock them.

They waited.

She stepped out from between the two buildings, a small figure with a shawl wrapped around her shoulders. She headed for the stables, twisting her head from side to side. She stepped into a pool of moonlight and her hair shone like the back of a crow's wing.

It was Clarita.

"Zak," she called in a loud whisper. "Are you there?"

"I am here," Zak replied, and Clarita ran toward him, her small feet flashing in the dark like tiny black birds.

A great sadness welled up in Zak as he thought about his father, about Corazon Mendez and her father, Paquito. And a little bright-eyed girl with a dazzling smile named Clarita. It hit him all at once, like a sledgehammer in the chest, and he felt something brush against his cheek. A memory, or his father's ghostly hand.

And the night turned cold and the moon painted silver baubles on the ground, lighting the small pebbles so that they gleamed like precious gems, flickered like so many lost souls left voiceless on the ruined earth of his past.

19

Clarita ran up to Zak and pulled on his leg.

"Let me up, let me up," she said in English.

Zak reached down and took her arm, slipped his foot out of the stirrup so that she could step into it. He hauled her up behind him.

"Quick," she said. "We must go. I will show you where."

Zak touched Nox's flanks with his blunted spurs and the horse stepped out of the barn.

"Turn here," she said, pointing to their left. "Go up the alley."

"What's going on, Clarita?" Zak asked as they passed behind the Silver Cup and headed for the next street. The cantina was dark. All the lights inside were out. Zak did not hear any music, or the rivers of conversation, rising and falling like a tidal surge of gabbing bullfrogs or the singsong conversations of sawing insects. The building was like a flaming cinder that had been doused in the sea. It was dead quiet, and Zak knew that wasn't natural or common. In the space of a few minutes, the saloon had closed and dozens of men and women had slipped silently into the night, as if ordered to do so, as if the desertion had been practiced, rehearsed, more than once, like a fire drill in a school or an "abandon ship" exercise on a passenger vessel during an ocean voyage.

"They come for you," she said. "Jorge and Ralph. They come to kill you."

"Where are we going?"

"To my father's house. Paquito wants to see you. Did you read my words on the note?"

"Yes," he said, turning his head so that she could hear him. "I remember."

"There is big trouble," she said in his ear. Her arms wrapped tightly around his waist as Zak put Nox into a gallop. He felt her soft breasts flattening against his back, smelled the scent of her perfume, felt the caress of her hair on the back of his neck. Jeff saw the burst of speed and spurred his own horse until he came up alongside Zak and Clarita. They reached the end of the alley.

That's when Nox ran into a tightly stretched rope that was strung across the opening. The rope struck the horse midway between the knees and hocks.

Nox tumbled, hurling Clarita and Zak to one side as he crashed to his side, legs flailing the air like a turtle on its back.

Jeff's horse hit the rope and went down, hurling Jeff over its head. He landed on his left shoulder. His neck snapped and his head smashed into the dirt.

Clarita went sprawling almost in the path of Jeff's horse. Zak hit on his belly. He felt the wind knocked out of his lungs, but he reached out for Clarita and pulled her away from eight hundred pounds of horse.

He covered her body with his own and drew his pistol. Nox righted himself and kicked until he got his legs underneath him, then stood up, dazed but not seriously injured.

"Git," Zak hissed as he pulled off his hat and waved it at Nox. The horse galloped into the dark street and turned the corner, running hard. His hoofbeats faded just as a shot rang out from the top of an adobe building across the street, directly opposite the rope that was still swaying to and fro, like a plucked string on some giant musical instrument.

Zak saw the muzzle flash, an orange flower that blossomed and died in an instant.

Jeff's horse screamed as the bullet smashed into its right shoulder, at the top of its leg. The wound exploded in blood and slivers of bone and the horse's leg collapsed.

"Put a bullet in that horse's head, Jeff, and crawl in behind it," Zak said, drawing a bead on the shooter.

Jeff crawled up to his horse, threw an arm over its neck to pin it down. The horse was thrashing in pain, blood streaming from the hole in its crippled shoulder. Jeff put his pistol barrel behind the horse's ear, cocked the weapon, and squeezed the trigger. The shot was muffled by the horse's head, and the animal stopped moaning and kicked twice, then lay still.

"Jesus," Jeff said and ducked his head as Zak fired at the figure on the rooftop.

The bullet was high and the man ducked.

Clarita started to whimper.

"Just lie still," Zak whispered to her.

"I do not want to die," she said.

"Then pray," he said.

"*Tengo miedo de morir*," she breathed, and Zak felt her trembling body nestling against his, and her hand clutching his shirt.

Out of the corner of his eye, Zak saw a figure emerge out of the darkness next to the nearest building, on Zak's right. The moon poured molten pewter light on the man's shoulders, glinted off the pistol in his hand.

Zak recognized him, just from his shape and the way he stood. He had stood the same way when he was at their table in The Silver Cup.

It was Jorge Dominguez.

Zak swung his pistol toward the man.

"You'd better stop right there, Jorge," Zak said.

Jorge stopped, went into a fighting crouch.

Zak heard a click as he cocked his pistol.

"Do you see this chisel in my hand, Jorge? It's chipping out something on a stone."

"What?" Jorge said.

"That's your headstone right in front of you. You take one more step and your name goes on it."

"You go to hell, gringo," Jorge hissed. He brought his pistol up.

It was a fatal mistake.

Zak's gun barked and fire exploded from the barrel, propelling a lead bullet at the speed of a thought straight toward Jorge's crouching figure.

The bullet struck Jorge just above his belt buckle with the force of a twenty-pound maul, driving him back on his heels as if he had been struck with a pile driver. He let out an ugly grunt and squeezed the trigger of his pistol. It bucked in his hand and drove a bullet straight into the ground in front of him. The pistol dropped from his hand and he grabbed his belly, trying to stanch the flow of blood that gushed out of him, with the stench of his bowels attached. A terrible odor filled the air.

"I do not see no chisel," he spat. "I do not see no fucking chisel."

"No, and you never will, Jorge," Zak said and fired again. The bullet ripped into Jorge's chest and ground his heart to a bloody pulp. He never uttered another word. He only sighed and slumped to the ground, his lips turning cherry red with the blood that bubbled from his mouth.

The man on the roof fired another rifle shot and the bullet smacked into Jeff's dead horse, raising dust and hairs in a gust. Jeff cracked off a shot and they heard the man scoot away from the edge of the roof, scraping his clothes on grit and adobe brick.

"Any more of 'em?" Jeff asked.

"We'll wait a minute," Zak said.

He heard more scraping, then a thud as the man jumped down from the roof at the back of the building. Then running footsteps.

"You wait here, Jeff," Zak said. "Watch over Clarita. Clarita, get over there with Jeff, behind that horse."

Zak jumped up and ran alongside the building where Jorge lay dead.

"Where do you go?" Clarita called after him.

"Be right back," Zak said, then disappeared down Esperanza Street.

Zak huddled against the storefront, listening. Then he saw what he was after, standing hitched to a rail in front of the next store. He sneaked up to the horse, unwrapped the reins, and was about to step around the rail when he heard a voice from across the street.

"You do not steal Jorge's horse."

Zak recognized the man but could not see him. The accent, the way he spoke.

It was Ralph Zigler, and the only thing between them was Jorge's horse.

"You have got a tombstone, also, Cody," Zigler said. "I write your epitaph on it, yah."

So, Zigler had heard what he'd said to Jorge.

He was probably the shooter up on the roof.

A damned bushwhacker.

A killer.

The street was empty. There was only one horse tied up in front of the saloon down the street. Probably Zigler's. He and Jorge had been left behind to lay a trap for Zak and Jeff. That rope across the end of the street. They had probably known Clarita would take them that way, and just waited in ambush. Two killers. One of them dead. The other just deadly. Deadly as hell.

Zigler laughed.

It was a dry guttural laugh. He was sure of himself. He was in shadow. Zak was bathed in dusty moonlight, out in the open.

The German's laugh told Zak where he was, but he could not see him.

If Jorge's horse moved, Zak knew he was a dead man.

He looked at the hitchrail. He looked at the horse. Just those two things between him and Zigler. Between him and certain death.

"Just one thing you forgot, Zigler," Zak said.

The seconds ticked by. Slow as a garden slug.

Seconds that seemed like an eternity.

Precious seconds that gave a man time to think.

Seconds that gave a man a little more time to live.

Or die.

— 20 —

Zak's hand tightened around the reins. Jorge's horse was still his only protection against Zigler, the only thing standing between them that was large enough to stop a bullet. His left arm rested on the hitchrail. He held his pistol in his right hand and his palm was beginning to sweat, even in the coolness of the evening.

Zigler was just waiting for the right moment to gun him down.

And Zak wasn't going to give him that moment. "Zigler," he called to the man across the street.

"Yah?"

"Do you still have that candle?"

"What candle?"

"The candle God gave you."

"You are crazy, Cody. Nobody to me gave the candle."

"Yes, God gave us all a candle. It burns only so long and then goes out."

"Oh, so you are a poet, yes?"

"No, Zigler, I'm the wind."

"*Was ist*? The wind?"

"Yes, I'm the wind that's going to blow your candle out."

With that Zak jerked hard on the reins, pulling the horse to his left, away from the hitchrail. Then he stepped around the rail and hugged the horse's rump, shielding himself from Zigler.

Zigler took a step toward the moving horse, lifting his pistol for a shot at Zak.

Zak heard the scuff of his boots, poked his head around the horse's backside and saw the glint of moonlight on the barrel of Zigler's pistol.

A split second to make a decision.

A fractured moment in a lifetime of moments.

Zigler moved his pistol from side to side, looking for an opportunity to fire it at Zak.

The horse sidestepped away from the pressure on its hip and Zak went into a crouch. He saw Zigler at the same time as the German saw him. Both fired their pistols almost at once.

Zigler's pistol roared. Sparks and flame burst from the barrel. The white smoke turned to gossamer in the moonlight. The bullet sizzled over Zak's shoulder like an angry hornet, smacked into the adobe wall behind him.

Zak aimed at a point just below Zigler's chin, allowing for the peculiarities of night vision. The bullet smashed into the center of Zigler's chest, splitting the breastbone, shearing off splinters of bone, smashing flesh and one lung to pulp before caroming off his spine and lodging in a rib. Zigler twisted into a grotesque shape as his legs gave way beneath him. He held on to his pistol, but could not summon the strength to thumb back the hammer. The hammer assumed the weight of an anvil, while his thumb was a useless appendage turned to soft sponge.

Zak ran over to the man, cocking his pistol. The horse sidled a few feet, turned its head to regard Zak's movements. But it stayed put, curious eyes glazed over with soft moonlight.

"*Gaaah*," Zigler said as he looked up at Zak. Smoke curled from the barrel of Zak's pistol, a diaphanous snake of light.

"That candle," Zak said. "It's about to go out."

"You bastard," Zigler croaked.

"Where's Pete?"

"Ha. You never catch him, Cody. They ride to the Jemez. Many guns to kill the American soldiers."

Zigler started to raise his gun.

Zak kicked it out of his hand, and it went spinning away, a metal whirligig.

"Too bad," Zak said. "I'd like to blow out his candle, too."

"I not die," Zigler said, his voice laced with arrogance.

"You don't feel the pain yet, Zigler. You're in shock. Like a rabbit. Pretty soon now you'll beg for me to put a bullet in your brain."

"I spit on you, Cody."

But Zigler could not summon up spit, nor did he have the strength to even purse his lips.

Zak walked over to Zigler's pistol. He picked it up and stuck it in his belt.

Zigler groaned in pain.

"That's the start of it, Herr Zigler. Just a little pinch of pain and then it'll tear through your body like a firebrand and you'll scream like a woman.

And nobody will hear you. Just me, and I won't give a damn."

"You are a bastard, Cody." And with those words, blood spurted out of Zigler's mouth. He choked on it and spat up a large gob that went down his chin like tomato pulp and stopped just above the hole in his chest.

Death might be merciful to Zigler after all, Zak thought. He was losing blood. That would weaken him. He might lose consciousness before the pain struck him. It was tough to watch a man die. Any man. But Zigler had chosen his path. Had he been lucky, it might have turned out differently. Zak himself might be lying in the dirty street, instead of Zigler.

Zigler moved as a sudden spasm rippled through his body. His feet kicked out and his legs jumped. His shoulders shook and his hands lost control, twitched like a pair of wounded animals.

"*Ahhh*," Zigler said. The groan was not deep in his throat, but more like air escaping. A fine spray of pink blood turned to silver mist and freckled his face.

"Any last request, Zigler? A final wish?"

"I wish you go to hell, Cody," Zigler gasped.

"Maybe I'll meet you there, Zigler."

"To hell you will go."

"You may already be there, Zigler, and just don't know it yet. If you feel a sharp prod in your back, that's probably the devil's pitchfork."

"Shit," Zigler said, and Zak knew he was losing reason. He didn't have enough blood in him to feed his brain. The little oxygen he was getting was just keeping his pump going. Zigler's pale blue eyes were almost empty. They were gleaming dully like nickels under the glaze of the moon. But they were not bright—more like tarnished silver.

Zak ejected the empty hulls from his pistol, put fresh cartridges in the chambers. Zigler watched him as a small animal would watch a venomous snake that's ready to strike.

Zak spun the cylinder, put the hammer on half cock.

"You shoot me now again?" Zigler said.

Blood oozed from the hole in his chest. It was not spurting, just eking out from the feeble beatings of his heart.

"No, Zigler. You have to die on your own."

"You have the cruel streak, Cody. *Gut.* My hate keeps me alive a little longer."

"Why waste another bullet on someone as worthless as you, Zigler?"

He said something in German that Zak could not quite hear.

Then Zigler's body contorted as he was struck by another sudden spasm.

Zak could read the pain on his face. His facial muscles tautened and his skin nearly matched the blondness of his hair. His red lips and pale eyes gave him the look of a man dug up from a grave, a man already dead.

Zigler closed his eyes as he fought against the intense pain. He opened his mouth as if trying to scream, but no sound came out. There was only a gurgle deep in his throat and another issuance of blood, a fine spray as he convulsed, and then strings of crimson that settled on his chest like sodden earthworms.

"So long, Zigler," Zak whispered under his breath.

He slipped his pistol back in his holster.

As he walked away, he heard a rattling sound in Zigler's throat, then a slight wheeze, followed by a deep silence.

He grabbed up the reins of Jorge's horse, a dark buckskin gelding, led him around the corner. He made sure his boots hit the ground hard enough for Vickers and Clarita to hear him coming.

"That you, Zak?" Jeff called out.

"Got you a horse, Jeff."

"We thought you were dead," Clarita said. "We heard the shooting."

"Who was it?" Jeff asked.

"Zigler."

"Good. Just those two, then?"

"I think so. Biederman either went with his men to the Jemez or sent Pete with them. A hundred or more, I figure."

"What are they going to do?"

Jeff and Clarita stood up, both brushing at their clothes.

Zak put two fingers in his mouth and gave out a piercing whistle.

"Mount up," he said to Jeff. "Clarita, you ride with him."

A moment later Nox gamboled up to them, reins trailing.

"To answer your question, Jeff, I think Leo's men are going to not only warn Narbona, but join him in trying to wipe out Loomis and his troops."

"We've got to warn Colonel Loomis."

"The soldiers rode out of the fort two or three hours ago," Clarita said. "That is what Pete told Leo. I heard them talking after you left."

"That fool," Vickers said. "He should have given us three days."

"Maybe he knows something we don't," Zak said. "I wouldn't fault Loomis just yet."

"What are we going to do? We have to warn Loomis what he's up against."

Zak climbed into the saddle, looked at Jeff.

"We're going to help Loomis if we can," Zak said. "If he goes into that country blind, then Leo's men and the Navajos will cut him to pieces."

"First, you must take me to my house, Zak," Clarita said. "It is very important that my father speak to you. It will not take long."

"It had better not," Zak said, "because we can't stay long. Jeff and I have a good ride ahead of us."

"I know," she said. "Come, I show you where we live."

Jeff took the lead, with Clarita holding out her arm every so often to point the way.

Zak thought of the time that had already passed, and tried to figure out where Loomis might be. He was pretty sure Pete and the others wouldn't attack him from the rear. No, they'd get ahead of Loomis somehow. They had the advantage. They knew the way to Narbona's camp. Loomis did not.

Perhaps, he thought, he and Jeff could beat both the army and Biederman's men into the Jemez. They would have to be like shadows—racing shadows. They would have to outwit Pete and his minions, and if they could catch up to Loomis, they might be able to reason with him, lead him through that terrible country and prepare him to do battle with a clever and powerful enemy.

It was a lot for two tired men who were running hours behind Loomis and probably an hour behind Pete Carmody.

Carlita cried out, "There. There's our house."

And there it was, a modest adobe building with moonlight on its porch roof, flowers in profusion, and a man standing in the lighted doorway. A man Zak remembered.

A man Zak knew.

⇥ 21 ⇤

Francisco "Paquito" Mendez wore his short gray hair like a monk's skullcap. His smile, wide and white and friendly, was as Zak had remembered it. His handshake when Zak entered his home was as strong as it ever was. The eyes, so brown they appeared almost black, were just as piercing, just as bright, as if lit by an inner fervor.

"Paquito," Zak said, "you look fit as a fiddle. This is my friend, Captain Jeff Vickers."

"Welcome to our poor home," Paquito said. "Please take seats. Do you wish a cup?"

"No," Zak said. "We can only stay a brief time. We must ride to the Jemez."

"Sit, sit," Paquito said. Both men removed their hats in deference to Clarita now that they were indoors.

Clarita took off her shawl, draped it over the back of an empty chair, and sat there, while Jeff and Zak seated themselves on the divan. Paquito sat in a baronial chair with a high back. It seemed to suit his judicial poise and confidence. Zak was not surprised that his friend was now a judge. Paquito had been outraged at the murder of Zak's father and had always voiced his opinions about injustice. He had decried the treatment of Mexicans, Indians, and poor white people in Taos and vowed to change what he could change before he died.

"I was sorry to hear about Elena," Zak said. "She was a good woman."

"The grief of losing Clarita's elder sister was too hard for her, I fear," Mendez said. "I think grief took her to heaven. She is with the angels."

Clarita crossed herself quickly, bowed her head. Elena was her mother, Paquito's wife.

"I was hoping Clarita would bring you here, Zak," Paquito said. "I know that you have met Leo Biederman and his wife, Minnie, and some of his henchmen."

"You know about Biederman?" Zak said.

"That is why I sent for you, Zak. I know a great deal about Leo Biederman, much to my misfortune."

"He is . . ." Zak started to say. Paquito held up his hand to stay him from further discussion.

"I will tell you about Leo," he said. Then he turned to Clarita and spoke in rapid Spanish. She nodded and rose from her chair.

"Excuse me," she said. "I will prepare coffee. My father insists that we all take a cup with him before you leave."

"Of course," Vickers said, ever the polite army officer. "We would be delighted."

Paquito smiled. Wanly, Zak thought. He had heard his friend mention coffee, but he had said something else to his daughter, something that was said with such celerity that Zak had trouble translating it. "*Ponga goats en las tazas de los dos caballeros.*" Or something like that. Something that did not make much sense, or that he may have misheard.

Clarita padded down the hall to the kitchen and Zak could hear the clatter of a pot, the rattle of kindling being thrown into a stove's firebox, and the clang of a stove lid banging into place.

"You look much tired, Zak," Paquito said. "And so do you, Captain Vickers."

"We'll sleep in the saddle if we must," Zak said. "Just what did you want to see me about, Paquito?"

"I think there are some things you must know about this man before you hunt him down. I have known Leo and Minnie for some time. They are dangerous people."

"I know that," Zak said.

"He is a greedy man. I have been watching him and have had to adjudicate some legal disputes involving him. Over some land filings involving Spanish land grants."

"I'm not surprised," Zak said.

"It became very clear to me, Zak, that Biederman is trying to grab up—and that is the term I use, even though it is not a legal one—all the land in the Rio Grande Valley. To this end, he has, shall we say, helped and encouraged the Navajo nation, certain members of that nation, to flee their reservations illegally, and attack farmers and ranchers on both sides of the Rio Grande, then file on their properties, which he has obtained illegally."

"I know some of this, I think," Zak said. "I also think he wants to destroy the army at Fort Marcy and the Presidio."

"That is true. So he wishes to draw the army into a fight, a dangerous fight, that the army cannot win."

"Yes, I know that, too." Zak told Paquito about his experience with Gregorio Delacruz, and what Narbona had said to him about telling the army.

"Yes. This Narbona is a very big man in the Navajo nation. He is almost like a god. The Navajos believe that he is their dead leader come back to life."

"A ghost," Zak said.

"Yes, but a live ghost with much power. Narbona—the real Narbona—died many years ago. This one has taken his name, which is against Navajo custom."

"I know that, too," Zak said.

"Did you also know that Leo's wife is the sister of Narbona? Leo calls her Minnie, but her name is Minerva."

"The Roman goddess," Zak said.

"Yes. The goddess of the hunt. She is a dangerous woman. She was the courier between Leo and Narbona. She wants her people to reclaim all of their ancient lands and drive all the whites and the Mexicans away."

"That is why Jeff and I must warn Colonel Loomis and try to stop Leo and Narbona."

"Just the two of you? That is a fool's errand, Zak. Listen to me. You must let the battle between Loomis and Narbona happen as if the fates had decreed it. You cannot stop them. Later, when Washington learns of the defeat of Loomis, they will send a bigger army and justice will be served."

"While hundreds of Americans spill their blood in the Jemez," Zak said.

Carlita came into the room bearing a wooden tray with four cups of coffee. She stopped before Jeff and handed him a cup, then handed another to Zak. She gave her father a cup and took the last one for herself. She set the tray on a small table in front of the divan and sat down.

Zak looked around the room, mulling over what Paquito had told him. There was a Spartan feel to the furnishings. In one corner, there was a small statue of the Virgin Mary with two votive candles burning in front of it. Zak thought it might be a shrine to Elena and Corazon, since there were two candles. There were pegs in the walls, a calendar hanging on one of them and a map of New Mexico on the other. There were no feminine touches, and Zak wondered if Carlita lived with her father or somewhere else. There was a fireplace and a mantel, with nothing on top except a small mirror that seemed out of place. It did not look like a place that saw much entertainment. There were books in a small bookcase. They looked like law books, with their thick leather bindings and ornate lettering on the spines.

He sipped the coffee, relishing its warmth and the lift it gave him. That lift was short-lived.

Jeff drank half of his cup and then reached out a hand to the armrest.

Zak saw the room go out of focus, the people and objects in it twisting into grotesque shapes. Then the room began to spin and he felt a rush of darkness rising up in his brain.

"You men need rest," Paquito said, and his voice sounded muffled and far away, as if Zak were hearing it with cotton stuffed in his ears.

"Paquito, what in hell did you do?" Zak asked, his own voice strangled in some silken web.

"I gave you the kind of drops sailors use when they shanghai a seaman. It will make you sleep a while, that's all. I do not want you and your friend to be killed."

Vickers tried to get up and toppled over. He fell headlong onto the floor, passed out cold.

Zak tried to bring Paquito into focus. The cup dropped out of his hands, fell to the floor, and shattered into shards.

Clarita rose from her chair to go to Zak, but her father held up his hand and shook his head.

"Damn you, Paquito," Zak said as the spinning moved from the room and into his brain. The darkness welled up again and everything went dark. He felt himself falling from a high cliff down into a dark sea that was turning red as blood.

Then he fell to one side and lay there like a stricken animal.

"We will put them in beds," Paquito said to his daughter.

"I want Zak to sleep in mine," she said.

"You have no shame, daughter."

She did not answer because Clarita knew her father was right.

When it came to Zak, the hero of her childhood, she had no shame.

None whatsoever.

22

Roaming through the dream corridors of his sub-conscious, Zak was a shadow gliding across emerald meadows where mule deer gamboled as he passed, and a beaver streamed a *V* of wavelets on a pond as it swam up from its domed den and streaked toward the shore, where a man, hip deep in the same silver water, oiled a trap with golden castoreum. The man had the face of Russell Cody before it transformed into the face of Paquito Mendez, then morphed into a grinning timber wolf.

The scene shifted to another, where his shadow was walking in a deserted landscape dominated by the sheer walls of red sandstone mountains, and he had a rifle in his hand. He entered a narrow canyon and saw the hunched figures of men with bows and arrows hiding behind immense red boulders, their faces painted for war. He started running and the sky filled with arrows. He turned and aimed his rifle, but it turned into a twisting snake and slithered from his hands. He felt a hot rain stinging his flesh and his shirt disintegrated, slid from his shoulders onto the ground, where it became a steaming puddle of mud and water. An Indian pounced on him, a female with long black tresses and ruby lips, eyes like fiery black diamonds. He began to burn inside, and the landscape evaporated into a warm mist that enveloped him. Then an ocean darkness, and he was swimming up from its depths, his lungs burning until he could reach air on the surface. He swam upward, out of sleep, flailing his rubbery arms, with nothing between him and death but a wine-dark sea.

He awoke to darkness—and a presence—his body naked, the bed beneath him soft and warm, a dark face next to his, a bare leg draped across his.

"Huh?" Zak said, groggy with sleepiness. "Where am I?"

"Zak, Zak," she cooed and the cobwebs in his mind thinned. "Love me, Zak. Love me."

"Carlita?"

"Yes, yes."

She peppered his face with warm kisses and he felt a hand brush across his chest, the fingers searching through the tangled wires of his hairs. Her lips pressed against his and he felt the heat of her. She slid atop him and her breasts flattened against his chest.

It was dark outside, still, and the faint light of the moon streamed through the window, too weak to define the room. The room seemed filled with a solid mist, frozen into immobility as if the light were frost and could stop time with its ghostly glow.

Carlita made love to him and he went to her willingly, let her satisfy herself before he turned her over on her back and took command, burying himself deep inside her until her back arched and she mewed like a kitten and then uttered a muffled scream. She collapsed into what the Mexicans called "the little death," sated and filled with him, and both came down from the heights like fallen birds, like swimmers floating on an ocean of air toward a distant, pillowy shore.

He slipped from her body and lay beside her, taking breaths into his lungs, struggling to get his bearings. He saw the room then, the adobe walls, dark frames on the walls, a single window filled with moonlight, a wardrobe against one wall, a table next to the bed, and shadows flitting like giant moths against the beamed ceiling.

"Carlita," he said when his breathing had returned to normal, "did Paquito knock me out?"

"Only to help you," she said.

"He should not have done that. I have to go."

"Yes, I know. But you slept, Zak. You rested and now you can go. But I fear for you. You are going where there is danger."

"Paquito had no right to do what he did. Where's Captain Vickers?"

"He sleeps in another room."

"Where are my clothes?"

He sat up, shaking out the streamers of cobwebs that still cloaked his brain. He felt as if there were heavy weights in his forehead, just above his eyes.

"I will get them for you," she said, sliding from the bed, a nymphlike creature out of a fairy tale, her naked body all curved and sinuous, limned with light until she vanished in shadow.

He heard the rustle of cloth and she reemerged, handing him his clothing. He sat there on the edge of the bed and dressed—pulled on his boots, strapped on his gun belt. He kept looking out the window, but he could not tell how close they were to the dawn.

"How long did I sleep?" he asked her when he was fully dressed.

She had slipped into a dress and put on sandals. She stood small and wanton in front of him, looking up at him.

"Maybe four hours. Are you rested, Zak?"

"I don't know. I'm still half asleep."

She laughed and he wanted her again, but pushed past her, toward the outline of a closed door.

"I've got to rouse Vickers," he said. "Point me the way."

"I will take you to him, Zak, and I will get coffee for you, heat some food for both of you."

"We've already lost valuable time," he said. "We've got to try and find Loomis before he rides into a death trap."

"Shh," she said. "There is time for all you want to do, Zak. You do not hurry. You go slow and you live long."

He followed her through the door to a little room, where Vickers was sawing wood, his snoring a raspy sound in the hollow of the adobe quarters. Zak pinched Jeff's nose and shook him awake. Vickers thrashed like a blind man as he rose to a sitting position.

"Where in hell am I?" he said.

Zak and Carlita both laughed.

"You might be in some part of hell if you don't get your ass out of that bed, Jeff."

"I must have passed out. God, I slept like a log. I thought . . ."

Zak stepped away from the bed.

"You were shanghaied, Jeff. Just like me."

"God, we should have . . ."

"Let's not fret over that now." Zak turned to Carlita. "That coffee hot?"

"Yes, come into the kitchen. There is a table and chairs there."

"I ought to punch your father," Zak said.

She slipped through the doorway and left a trail of delicate perfume in her wake.

Paquito was already up and dressed, seated at the table. A pair of oil lamps lit the kitchen. Clarita poured coffee.

"I grained and watered your horses while you slept," Paquito said. "They are saddled and ready for you. There is food in your saddlebags, some meat and tortillas and beans that Clarita fried. Your canteens are filled."

"Paquito," Zak said, "you are every bit the bastard my father said you were."

"Did Russell say that about me?"

"He said you were stubborn and ornery."

"Ah, then we did know each other, Russell and I."

"I ought to lay you out for putting those drops in our coffee."

"I did not put them there. Clarita did."

"What was it she put in?" Jeff asked.

"I believe it is called chloral hydrate. Some people call it—what is the word, Clarita?"

"A Mickey Finn," she said.

Paquito laughed.

"Yes, a Mickey Finn. I think he was some kind of Irish brute."

"My head feels fuzzy inside," Jeff said.

"That will wear off in time," Paquito said. "The coffee will wash away the spider webs."

"I ought to pour mine all over your head, Paquito," Zak said. "You cost me valuable time."

"Listen to me, Zak," Paquito leaned close. Steam from the coffee spiraled up from his cup in a lazy pigtail. "Clarita told me she heard Leo tell Pete Carmody to have some men wait for you in ambush in case you got away from Jorge and Ralph. If you had ridden away last night, you both would be dead now."

Zak turned to Clarita.

"Did you hear that?"

"Yes. That is why I had to get away, to warn you, to keep you from getting shot. In the daylight, you can see. They will not ambush you."

"Tell me, Clarita," Zak said, "just what were you doing in that cantina anyway? Do you work there? Do you—"

She laughed and pressed a finger against his lips to silence him.

"I work for my father. When you first saw me, I was there to deliver papers, legal documents, for Leo to sign. They said he would be back in the evening, so I stayed there, hoping you would come back, too."

"I thought maybe you and Leo—"

"No, you must not think such thoughts. Besides, if Leo tried to kiss me, Minnie would cut my throat."

"She has done that, you know," Paquito said.

"What? Cut Clarita's throat?"

"No, she cut the throat of a woman who wanted to bed Leo."

"And she got away with it?"

Paquito shrugged.

"The witnesses all claimed she acted in self-defense."

"You heard the case?"

"It never went to trial. But it would have been the same. No evidence to convict her of a crime."

"She did it again, too," Clarita said. "Not to a woman, but to a man."

"What?" Jeff said.

"A man who worked for Leo got mad and came gunning for him," Paquito said. "Minnie flew at him like a puma and clawed his face. Then she took the knife she keeps under her skirt and stabbed him in the stomach. Then as he was on his knees, she slashed open his throat."

"I suppose that was self-defense, too," Zak said.

Paquito smiled. "What do you think?"

"I think the law in Santa Fe is seriously wounded, if not entirely dead."

Clarita served little bundles of *carne asada, frijoles refritos*, and chopped onions to Jeff and Zak. They ate hurriedly and drank another cup of coffee each. They grabbed their rifles and walked out into the morning.

The dawn was just breaking when they rode away from Paquito's house. Zak looked back and waved to Clarita. He felt a pang of regret, a small sadness that he was leaving.

"At least we'll have the sun at our backs all morning," Jeff said as they cleared the town, crossed the Taos road, and headed for the Rio Grande.

"And in our eyes all afternoon," Zak said.

He knew they had a ride ahead of them, and

little chance of stopping Loomis from riding into the Jemez and facing armed men, white and Indian, bent on destroying him and his troops. And the worst part was that Loomis and his troops would probably never see the enemy. They would be hidden behind rocks, up on the rimrock, sitting in brush, or hiding almost anywhere in that rugged country.

"Do we have a chance of catching up to the colonel before he walks into a trap?" Jeff asked after they had forded the Rio Grande."

"I doubt it, Jeff. Not unless every trooper's horse gets a rock stuck in its shoe."

"What are we going to do, then? Do you have a plan?"

"I don't know, Jeff. A plan is something you make when you know what lies ahead."

"And you don't know what lies ahead, do you, Zak?"

"Yes, I know. But I sure as hell don't want to talk about it."

The two men rode into the Jemez late in the afternoon, following the tracks of both Leo and his men and Loomis and his troops. They rode into the desolation and immense silence of that country, like wanderers in an unknown country, the sheer bluffs of iron-red monuments rising above them like the walls of a fortress, the silence so deep their own thoughts boomed in their minds as loud as thunder.

23

Amid the maze of tracks Zak saw the wheel ruts. He tried to decipher the strength of the two opposing forces, but could only come up with a rough estimate.

"I reckon Loomis fielded a company," Zak said. "Maybe eighty men or so."

"More like a hundred, Zak."

"And two mountain howitzers."

"Yes. Brass twelve-pounders. Might make a difference."

"And Biederman, I figure, took eighteen or twenty men with him."

"At least a dozen, looks like," Vickers said.

"Maybe enough, depending on how large Narbona's force is."

"How many Navajos did you count in that valley camp, Zak?"

"At least fifty fighting men."

"If that's the only camp, Loomis might have a chance."

Zak wasn't that optimistic, but he didn't say anything to Jeff. The Navajos had the advantage of terrain and they probably had at least two camps, perhaps more. They knew the country; Colonel Loomis did not. And Loomis would have a difficult time wrestling those two howitzers up to high ground, where they would be most effective. The mules would struggle to pull over two hundred pounds of metal up that same rugged mountain where he and Jeff had spotted the Navajo camp.

There were cart tracks, too, weaving through the tracks of the cannon.

"At least Loomis had sense enough not to bring four-wheeled wagons," Zak said.

"He's carrying powder and ball, probably cartridges, too. He'd want to split the supplies up, not put all his eggs in one basket."

"If he makes a stand, he'll have all his eggs in one basket," Zak said, worrying his lower lip with his teeth. He saw a golden eagle float by, riding the thermal currents, sailing across a land basking in heat, looking for that one little tail twitch, ear flick, or glint of eyes to find its prey. Loomis was doing much the same thing on the ground. The eagle could see for miles. Loomis would be lucky to see more than a couple of hundred yards ahead. And what he'd see would be conical hills, each one a potential hiding place for men with rifles.

They kept the horses at a good pace. The gelding Jeff rode was a sturdy horse with good legs and bottom, a strong chest. Nox stepped out like a champion with his ground-eating gait. Sweat sleeked his black hide until his coat shone like polished ebony. His tail swished at flies and his neck trembled under his dark mane as the insects sank their needle-like probes into his flesh, gorging on salt and blood.

"Zak," Jeff said late that afternoon, as he dabbed his forehead with his handkerchief to soak up the excessive sweat, "don't you think we ought to rest these horses for a while?"

"We'll be at a higher altitude come nightfall," Zak said.

"Maybe on two dead horses."

"It will be cool then. They'll probably whicker for a blanket before midnight."

"You ever command any troops?"

"No, never did."

"I can see why. What did you do for General Crook, anyway? Conduct forced marches?"

"I was a scout."

"A scout? You mean you didn't ride with the cavalry?"

"Nope. Never did. Cavalry had to catch up with me."

"And did they?"

"Not unless I wanted them to," Zak said.

They rode into the Jemez just at dusk, when the western sky was on fire, the clouds burning to a crisp above the snowcapped peaks. As the night came on, the flies stopped nagging the horses and biting the men's necks, and a cool breeze blew, drying up their sweaty faces and ruffling the moisture out of their billowing shirts.

"Now can we stop and rest, Zak?"

"We know where Biederman and Loomis are going," Zak said. "No need to scour the ground for their tracks."

"In a few minutes, it'll be black as pitch. We won't be able to see a damned thing."

"Won't have to see anything. I can smell them already."

"You can?"

"The air is full of messages, Jeff. You just have to sort them out."

"I don't smell anything but my own sweat and my horse's."

"There's other sweat."

Zak heard Jeff sniffing the air and suppressed a smile. He could follow the tracks in the dark. There was the smell of horse dung, for one thing, and for another, there was the earthy scent of men and horses blowing toward them. To his keen sense of smell it was like riding toward a stockyard in Kansas City or Denver—almost overpowering.

The small, conical hills began to appear, like mushrooms pushing up through dank soil in some dark cave, and still, Zak rode on, Jeff following him, as lost to his surroundings as a blind man. Zak glanced at Nox's ears every so often. They were like an insect's antennas, twisting one way, then another, searching for every alien sound, and his rubbery nostrils flexed like an elephant's trunk, scouring the air for vagrant scents. Zak noticed a change in Nox's gait: His hindquarters were drifting slightly to the right so that he was almost sidling along every so often, as if to be able to turn on a dime and gallop away from danger, or go on the attack if some large animal, like a puma, came at him from that direction. These were subtle movements, but Zak knew from experience not only how to read them but also how to interpret them. He was one with his horse, and the stock of his rifle was within easy reach, as was the butt of his pistol. He held the reins—actually a single rein, one loop, in his left hand—so that he could drop it and not have to reach down to retrieve two ends when he needed to control Nox.

The silence of the night and the rugged country was broken when they heard the roar of a cannon less than a half mile ahead. There was a mushrooming flash of light and the crackle of rifle fire, followed by another roar of thunder as a second cannon loosed its lethal leaden ball in a river of fire and brimstone.

"Those are the howitzers!" Jeff exclaimed. "Loomis is engaging the enemy."

"Calm down, Captain," Zak said. "The neighbors are quarreling."

"What?"

"Worse thing you can do is walk into a domestic quarrel, man and wife fighting, or two neighbors going at it tooth and nail."

"What in hell are you talking about? That's cannon fire and Sharps rifles. Loomis is in a fight."

"And if you ride into it, you're liable to get a lead ball square in your brisket. Let's just go real slow and see how long this lasts." Zak reined Nox to a halt.

Jeff rode up alongside him, pulling his rifle from its scabbard.

Zak reached over and grabbed Jeff's wrist. "Put that back and sit tight," he said.

Reluctantly, Jeff let the rifle slide back into its sheath. "What if the Navajos come at us, or Biederman's bunch?"

"They can see about as well as you in this darkness, Jeff."

"Shit. We're missing out on the fight."

"And you're out of uniform, Captain Vickers. Just be patient. Listen."

They heard more rifle fire and saw small flashes of orange light. Zak looked up at the hills and saw some sparks, like the winking glow of cigarettes that lasted only a fraction of a second.

Horses whinnied and they could hear the muffled shouts of men, frantic hoofbeats, and the creak of wagons.

Zak pictured it in his mind.

Loomis had been ambushed, probably while he was making camp, and now his men were scrambling for cover, firing blindly into the hills. He did not think it a full-fledged attack, but only harassing fire from an enemy who knew the country and wanted to put some fear into the hearts of the soldiers.

The firing died down. There was a single rifle shot. Then another. Then silence.

"Does Loomis use a password?" Zak asked.

"I don't know. Probably. Why?"

"Because we're going to ride up into his camp and I don't want to get shot out of the saddle."

"Good point, Zak."

"Just follow me."

Zak took a white handkerchief out of his back pocket, slipped his rifle from its boot, and tied the kerchief just behind the front blade sight.

He held the rifle upright, the butt resting on his calf, and rode forward, keeping Nox at a walk so that his hoofbeats didn't sound threatening.

A few moments later a man's voice challenged Zak and Jeff.

"Who goes there?" A tremor in the voice.

Zak waggled the rifle. The handkerchief flew back and forth like a wounded gull flapping its wings.

"Cody and Captain Vickers," Zak said.

"Advance and be recognized." This was another voice, one more firm and self-assured.

Zak prodded Nox with his spurs and the horse ambled forward. Jeff rode next to him, one hand on the stock of his rifle.

"Halt."

Zak and Jeff halted.

"Who are you?" The second voice.

"Zak Cody and Captain Jeff Vickers."

There were whispers between at least two men as Jeff and Zak waited.

"All right. Advance real slow. That a white flag?"

"It's a handkerchief," Zak said. "We don't want to be shot by a nervous sentry."

"That you, Captain Vickers?" another voice called out.

"Yes. That you, Nelson?"

"Yes, sir. I guess it's okay to ride up. Nobody's going to shoot you."

"As you were, Nelson. There's two of us. We're riding up."

Three men walked toward them, two with rifles to their shoulders, a third with his rifle held hip high.

"Take me to Colonel Loomis," Zak said.

"Take us both to the colonel," Jeff said.

"Yes, sir, Captain. Follow me." It was Lieutenant Ronald Nelson, and he issued instructions to the other two men and walked toward a mass of men and horses, holding ground under the sheer wall of a massive bluff that jutted up into the stars like some ancient battlement.

Men were lying on the ground in a semicircle, defending the position. They were flanked by the two howitzers. The ammunition carts stood at equidistance from one another, guarded by standing men with rifles at the ready.

"Colonel Loomis, it's Lieutenant Nelson, sir, with two riders, Captain Vickers and somebody named Cody."

Loomis walked up out of the shadows, a saber flashing in his hand.

"Dismount, men," he said, "or risk being shot down by snipers."

Zak and Jeff dismounted.

"Cody, you're the last person I expected to see out here," Loomis said. "You, too, Captain Vickers. Right now, you're both in the way. Captain, you're out of uniform, and Cody, I guess I broke my promise to you."

"I didn't come here to quarrel with you, Colonel. Any casualties?"

"Two men wounded slightly. The bastards jumped us just after dark. I let 'em have some cannon fire and drove them off."

"You didn't drive them off, Colonel," Zak said. "They're watching us right now, just waiting for the light of day to swoop down on you and kill every man jack in uniform."

"Oh, Cody, damn it. What in hell do you know?"

"Not much, maybe, Colonel, but a damned site more than you do right now."

Loomis glared at Cody but held his tongue. There were men around, listening to every word. They were worried men, some frightened, most of them bewildered, and Loomis knew that they looked to their commander for guidance. He let out a breath and stepped close to Cody.

"Maybe you and I had better have a private talk, Colonel Cody."

"Fine with me, Colonel. Lead the way."

The two men walked behind a small hill, leaving Jeff and Nelson behind.

"I'd put that saber back where it came from, Loomis," Zak said. "In the starlight it shines like a silver lantern. You could lose an arm. That would make a fine trophy for Narbona to take back to his lodge."

Loomis looked down at the sword in his hand.

At that moment it began to dawn on him that he was no longer in charge.

He sheathed the saber. It made a hissing sound as it slid back into its leather scabbard. It sounded, in the darkness, like a metallic snake. But it took the starlight with it and now the two men stood in the relative safety of shadow and hunkered down to talk, men of war conferring on a silent battlefield, as soldiers have always done when the deadly firing dies down just after nightfall.

High up on the hill, a great horned owl trumpeted its throaty call.

Only Zak knew that it wasn't an owl, but a Navajo warrior with perfect pitch.

24

There was another owl call from a different hill. This one was in a lower key, more deep-throated than the other, even lower-pitched, and it carried the oddly seductive tonal quality of a mating call.

But Zak was not fooled.

A human throat had made that second call, and the first one as well.

The Navajos were hiding on two hills, waiting. Watching.

"Colonel," Zak said, "you're in a tight spot here."

"I know that, Cody."

"I can get you out, but you have to do exactly as I say. Do you have a problem with that?"

"No. You're the Indian fighter, Cody."

"You're up against white men, too, Colonel."

"Look, call me Jeremiah, or Jerry, will you?"

"If you call me Zak."

"All right, Zak. What do you want me to do?"

"The first thing is to shuck that saber you're packing on your belt. Bury it in blankets. You'll rattle like a box full of washers once you start climbing that hill."

"What hill?"

"Right now, Jerry, you're backed up against a wall of rock. It'll be like standing in front of a firing squad when the sun comes up tomorrow. But you can ease around that limestone face and there'll be another hill just to the west of it. You and your men will be protected by that wall of stone while you do this."

"How do you know there's a hill west of my position?"

"Because I rode through this country the other day. Listen. Let your men slip away in small groups, meet you on the backside of this big bluff. Then, proceed west to this other hill. It'll be the smallest one, but you can leave men there to protect your flanks and rear while you take those howitzers up the next hill, which is right next to it, connected by a wide saddleback."

"I'll follow you, Zak."

"Once you have the high ground, you can defend yourself. Set your cannon to fire down along that defile and place your men all along the ridge so that you can lay down fire over a large area."

"You sound as if you're not going to be on this expedition."

"I'm not," Zak said.

"What are you going to do?"

"I'm going to leave my horse and rifle with your men and go on foot into the trees on those two hills."

"Just by yourself?"

"Jerry, this is the way I fight. I have a pair of Apache moccasins in the bottom of my saddlebag. I'll pack my pistol and my knife. I want to lessen the odds against you."

"One man against so many?"

Zak drew in a breath, let it out through his nostrils.

"Sometimes one man can do more than a company in country like this."

"You're taking a big risk."

"Let me worry about that. Now, get your men and cannon up on that second hill. There's a Navajo camp just beyond it, but they can't come up that way without great cost. So that flank is protected. To your rear are more canyons and ravines that will be difficult for the Navajos and white men to negotiate without suffering heavy losses. So you'll have only one flank to protect and they'll think twice before mounting an attack from that side."

"Sounds like a feasible plan," Loomis said.

"It's going to be tough for you to get those howitzers up those hills. Better start now. Send maybe half your company ahead by twos and threes, then haul the first cannon, send more men and then the other cannon, and finally, the last of your men."

"Got it," Loomis said.

"Good. Let's get going, then."

The two men walked back to the camp. While Loomis issued orders through his lieutenants, Vickers and Bullard came up to Zak, who told them of the plan.

"You don't want us to go with you?" Vickers said. "Sergeant Bullard here said he'd follow you to hell."

"No, I'm going alone. Randy, you take care of my horse and rifle."

"Yes, sir," Randy said.

"Keep the reins looped over the saddle horn. Make sure my rifle rides tight in its boot. Don't hobble him. He'll stay with you if I tell him to."

"He will?"

"But I want to be able to whistle him to me if I need him. So keep him in sight, but let him roam free. Can you do that for me?"

"Sure can, Zak."

Zak spoke to the horse, patting him on his withers.

"Stay, Nox, stay," he said.

Zak handed Randy the reins and dug into one of his saddlebags. He pulled out a pair of beadless moccasins and a red-and-yellow headband.

"Where'd you get those?" Jeff asked, pointing to the moccasins.

"A present from Cochise."

Zak sat on a rock and took off his boots and hat. He slipped into the moccasins and wrapped the headband on and tied it in the back so that both ends dangled down the back of his neck.

"You look like a white Apache," Jeff said. "Damned if you don't."

"Yes, sir," Bullard said, "you sure as hell do."

"Once I get where I'm going," Zak said, "I hope I'm invisible."

Men began moving along the face of the sheer bluff and Zak melted into the night, slipping across the flat to the base of a hill. He did not climb there, but crept in a circle around it to the back side. He heard the wheels of the carts as they rolled over rocks. The howitzers rumbled on their wheels and then he was in the silence on the back side of the hill. He carried neither food nor canteen, but only his Colt and a full cartridge belt, his knife, and the clothes he wore on his back.

Zak made no sound as he ascended the hill. He avoided dry branches and did not dislodge any stones. With each step he took, he felt the ground with the sole of his foot before putting his full weight on it. It was slow going, but he angled up the slope, using the scrub pines and juniper bushes for cover. He crept along, hunched over, stopping every few seconds to listen. When he got close to the summit, he heard the soldiers moving down on the flat. He also heard whispers from a clump of trees off to his left.

He closed in on the whisperers, taking special care with each step. He made no sound with his moccasined feet and he did not brush against branches or scrape the bark of any tree.

He squatted as he came close, closed his fingers around the staghorn grip of his knife. He eased it out of its scabbard, so slowly the sharp blade made no whisper against the smooth leather. When it was in his hand and out of its sheath, he crabbed forward until he could see two figures huddled together behind a jumble of rocks.

It took some time for his eyes to define each man, but their heads moved and one or the other would rise up to peer over the rocks at the soldiers down below.

The two men spoke in a language Zak did not understand.

Navajo.

But they interspersed their talk with Spanish words, like *soldado* and *ejército*, and once he heard the name Narbona, and a few minutes later, Minerva. Minnie Biederman. Narbona's sister. So, she was with her husband, and maybe with her brother. Where were the white men? He listened for a long time. The two Navajos did not talk much, but they kept rising to peer down at the progress of the soldiers. He wondered if they were the only lookouts on the hill, or if they were just the two at the highest point.

He strained to hear anyone else who might be close.

He heard no talk, no sound.

He crept closer until he was only a few feet behind the two men. They did not look over their shoulders. They were intent on their spying.

Finally, when the noises of the soldiers and the rolling stock grew faint and then vanished, one of the men spoke above a whisper. Zak could not understand him. The man used no Spanish, but the other one listened and then rose to his feet and stole away off to his left. Zak could hear his footfalls for several seconds and they faded into a soundless vacuum. The other man stood up and stretched his arms. He continued to look downward.

That's when Zak made his move.

He rose to a crouch and lunged toward the standing man. He grabbed him across the mouth with his left hand and forced him to the ground. He put the tip of his blade against the man's throat. The man dropped his rifle, but Zak caught it with his foot and eased it to the ground. The man wore no sidearm, only a knife on his belt. Zak left it where it was.

"*Hablas la lengua?*" Zak asked.

He loosened his hold slightly on the man's mouth, enough to allow him to speak.

"A little," the Navajo replied in Spanish.

"Where is Narbona?"

"He has gone. He is in the hills. You will not find him."

"No, but you will. Tell Narbona the Shadow Rider is here. Tell him the Shadow Rider is coming to kill him."

The man grunted and struggled. Zak pricked the soft skin of his neck with the tip of his blade.

"I will cut your throat if you fight me," Zak said. "You will live if you carry my words to Narbona."

"Narbona will kill me."

"You can die here or at Narbona's hand. I give you that choice."

"I will carry your words to Narbona."

"If you look behind you, I will be the shadow you see. Do you understand?"

"I understand."

"Go, then. Go to Narbona."

Zak jerked the man's knife from its scabbard and gave him a kick. The man trotted off in the same direction as his companion had gone, his *bandolera* rattling against his bare chest as he ran, leather slapping against skin, cartridges clicking together like tiny castanets.

Zak threw the knife down the slope, heard it strike a bush and then clank on a stone. He threw the rifle down over some bushes. It was an old Spencer carbine. The rifle clattered over pebbles, then skidded to a stop.

He drew a breath, held it, stepped back into the

trees and deep shadows. He listened. He waited, then angled left in the same direction the two Navajo braves had taken. Again, he moved, slow and wraithlike, through the scrub pines, staying well off the path the two Navajos had taken, but keeping it within eyesight. He checked every suspicious clump of shadow and every hollow, every large rock, every bush.

He had gotten a good look at the man he'd held at knifepoint. He would remember his face and the crimson breechclout he wore, the beaded moccasins. He heard nothing as he began to descend the hill and, as he started climbing the next, he began to think he was all alone.

The climb was steep and he stopped to catch his breath.

That's when he heard the soft crunch of a footfall on sandy ground.

Zak froze and crouched low, his feet apart and flat on the ground, his legs beneath him like a pair of springs. He held the knife low, under the calf of his leg so that the blade would not shine in the faint spray of starlight.

Silence for a few moments.

Then another footfall, close by. Heavy breathing. Another crunch—and it was not made by a moccasin, but a boot.

A figure loomed in front of him, advancing a careful step at a time. Step, wait, step, wait. The man was stalking him, Zak was sure of that. He crouched still lower, but was prepared to spring up if the man got within striking distance.

"Largos, you there?" the man said. Zak did not recognize the voice, but he knew it was a white man.

Zak made no sound.

The man took two more steps and Zak saw him framed against the stars, a rifle in his hand, his pistol tied low on his leg. He did not recognize him, but knew he must be one of Biederman's men.

The man saw the crouched shadow and started to raise his rifle.

Zak lunged at him, his blade pointed at the man's gut.

The rifle came to the man's shoulder.

An owl hooted nearby, sounding like a rooster with a sore throat, the same cadenced cry, pitched two octaves lower than a barnyard fowl. An owl that was not an owl, but a very good imitation. The stars behind the man streaked across the sky, spun wildly just above his head. Then Zak could see them no more.

He only saw the blackness of the man's midsection.

He was close enough that he could smell the man's fear.

25

When time cracks its whip, a small square of universe can bend and twist until a man feels as if he walks through a quagmire of quicksand or is hurtling off a cliff into an interminable abyss at the speed of lightning. And sometimes, time becomes all jumbled up, going fast, then so slow it seems to crawl. Time, someone once said, is God's way of keeping everything from happening all at once.

But now, everything seemed to be happening in a single whip crack of light.

Zak drove the blade of his knife deep into the gut of the man with the rifle. He struck him with the force of a pile driver cut loose from its moorings. The blade went in hard and Zak's momentum added power to his thrust so that he was sure the tip of the knife struck hard bone, the supple bone of the spinal column.

The man doubled over and Zak carried his weight on his back for a second or two, until they both went down in a heap. There was a terrible gush of blood all over Zak's back, and the smell of the man's bowels emptying. The heavy Henry rifle rang on stone like a blacksmith's hammer on an iron anvil, and hands tore wildly at his gun belt, fingers clawing for purchase, until the two rolled like a pair of intertwined tumbleweeds kicked into motion by the sudden force of a prairie twister.

Zak twisted the blade inside the mushy innards of the man and heard parts of him screech like pulled nails from an oak plank, while others snapped and flapped like springs made of melting rubber. The blade traveled in a short arc and parted flesh and skin, opening the man's side up like a gutted watermelon.

With the knife freed from its carnage, Zak reared up and rammed the blade square into the man's neck, slicing through his Adam's apple, releasing a freshet of blood that spewed a scarlet fountain onto the man's chest and onto the ground. The man sagged into death, a lifeless corpse destined to return to dust.

Zak wiped the blade of his knife on the dead man's trouser leg, slid it back into its sheath. He retrieved cartridges from the man's shirt pockets and picked up the Henry. It was heavy, a Yellowboy, with its brass receiver. The magazine was full, the rifle cocked. Zak eased the hammer down to half cock and padded away, following the contour of the hill. He headed toward the place where he had heard that owl call, treading quietly with his moccasined feet.

He heard the call again. Twenty, thirty yards away, on the opposite slope. He began to climb, grabbing the trunks of scrub pine, pulling himself up, zigzagging to take advantage both of the cover and the trees for his handholds. He listened, heard the sound of breathing a dozen yards from him. He crouched down and crabbed forward, a half foot at a time.

The stalking was easy. He came upon a lone Navajo sitting on a flat rock in plain sight, his back to him. He was looking down at an empty flat. All of the soldiers, carts, and cannon were gone, and nobody was walking through the temporary camp to check for lost objects.

The Navajos were biding their time, possibly waiting until morning before seeking out the soldiers, mounting an attack. Or they were moving around on other hills that Zak could not see. If so, they were noiseless, as was he. The brave below him cupped his hands to his mouth and gave the owl call again.

Zak let him finish before he laid the Henry down and snuck down toward his prey, knife in hand. His arm moved like a spring, and he buried the knife in the center of the Navajo's back, twisted it, then quickly pulled it free of bone and wet flesh and sliced the blade across the man's throat. He held out his left arm and the brave fell into it. Zak eased him down on his side. The man was dead, his Spencer carbine by his side. Zak let it lie. He carried the Henry with him. It made a good walking stick for the steeper parts of the hills, and if he needed a long weapon, he'd have it with him.

He climbed to cover atop the hill and sat there for a long time listening. He heard an answering owl call from far away, pondered its meaning. Was it an answering call to the one he'd just witnessed, or did it carry some new message to the Navajos roaming the hills or sitting like sentinels, awaiting the dawn?

He sat there, pondering what he had accomplished, what the results showed him. Not much. There were few rifles on that particular hill. Where were Biederman, Minnie, and Pete? Where were Narbona and Largos, the main body of whites and Navajos? They were not on the hill where he sat. And they were probably not gathered in any numbers on the next hill.

Narbona probably figured the soldiers would bivouac and stay put in one place. Easy pickings. But now the soldiers were on the move and protected, for the time being, from another attack. It was difficult to fight a battle in the darkness. And the Navajos believed in spirits and did not like to hunt or do battle at night. If they did make another strike, it would be just at dawn, or shortly thereafter.

He was getting nowhere, picking off a man at a time. He wanted to get close to either Narbona or Biederman, or both.

Cut the heads off two snakes, if he could.

The night was his ally, but he was as blind as anyone else. The moon had not yet cleared the high mountains and there was only the Milky Way and billions of stars shedding a faint light on the earth. And the mountains, the hills, were perfect hiding places for animals and humans. Every clump of brush, every cactus, every rock, and every tree robbed the senses. Everything with a shape looked like something else. Unless something moved, all shadows were the enemy, each shape potentially dangerous.

He could wander the night and get nowhere, or he could continue on toward the Navajo camp he and Bullard had spotted. If people were moving around, he would see them. If all were sleeping, he could get close and perhaps learn the enemy's plans when daylight came. He had the advantage at the moment. He knew where the soldiers were heading. He knew where one of the Navajo camps was, and he knew there were enemy sentries here and there, in singles, twos, and maybe threes.

That was enough for now, Zak decided. He drew in a long breath and began his stalk up the adjacent hill, varying his route so that he did not ascend in a straight line.

To his surprise, he did not encounter any sentinels during his ascent. He would have expected Biederman or Narbona to have sentries posted all along that exposed area. He thought they must be pretty confident that no soldiers would attempt to climb those hills during the night.

One or both of them were pretty arrogant, Zak thought, and when he reached the crest, he realized that he was alone on top of that hill. But when he began his descent on the other side, he heard human voices and froze in his tracks.

He could not understand the words, but knew they were in English, spoken by Americans. Curious, he crept closer. Again, he was hunched over so that he was no higher than any of the trees or plants. He stopped every few steps to listen. The conversation died and then rose up again. It was not really a conversation as such, but more like two people standing together making comments every so often.

"Hell of a place to spend the night," one of the men said, and Zak could hear him without strain.

"You ask me, Biederman's a little touched. Maybe not plumb loco, but touched."

"Ain't him, so much. It's that Injun woman of his. The Minié ball."

The other man laughed.

Zak did not recognize the voices, but he suspected they were two of Biederman's henchmen, part of his "army."

"Yair, she's a strange one. Them eyes, like a pair of gun barrels."

"You seen her brother?"

"That Narbona?"

"Umm, that one. He's got mean writ all over him."

"I seen him talkin' to Leo. They looked like a couple of pollyticians jabberin' away."

"Yep, that's what they look like and what they are. Old Narbona thinks he's goin' to get back all his Navvyho land, and Leo means to keep it for hisself."

"You better not let Leo hear you say that, Red."

Red laughed.

"Or Narbonny neither, I reckon."

The men were silent for a few moments and Zak crept closer.

Maybe, he thought, these two were some kind of rear guard. If so, then neither Narbona nor Leo expected any threat from this particular direction.

The two men stood near the bottom of a small hill. He could see their cigarettes glowing in the dark.

They were close, but they were in a bad spot for Zak to stalk them. They might not hear him descend to their level, but they would surely see him when he stood up to brace them.

Zak waited. He was concealed behind some juniper bushes and a small pile of stones. He watched the cigarettes float in the darkness, trailing sparks, scrawling arcs and geometric lines as the men moved their hands. He could not see their faces, only their dark silhouettes, their hats and, when they puffed, a faint light on their lips.

Then he heard rocks falling. The two men turned around, dropped their cigarettes to the ground.

"Pete, that you?" one of the men called out.

"Yeah, Farris. Red still with you?"

"Naw, he run off," Farris said, with a sarcastic twang to his voice.

"Don't get smart, Farris. Red, you see anything?"

"Nope, Pete. Nary."

"Well, you two boys go on up to the camp, get yourselves some grub."

Pete hove into view, a lanky stick figure scrambling down the slope of a little hill, a sliver of light glinting off his rifle. He joined the two men. One of them offered him a cigarette. He took it, and the other man, Red or Farris, struck a match and lit it for him. Zak saw their faces in the blaze of the match for only a second or two. But he recognized Pete.

"You goin' to stay here, Pete?"

"For a little while. I think them soldier boys have gone beddy-bye for the night."

"Yeah, it's real quiet."

"They're probably suckin' on their sugar tits," Red said. Zak knew which one he was because he had seen a lock of his hair when he lit the match.

All three men laughed.

"Go on, get your asses up the hill and keep goin' another mile. You'll see a campfire."

"What's Leo doin'?" Farris asked.

"Humpin' his woman," Pete said.

Red and Farris laughed. The laughter was bawdy.

"Any Injun women in our camp?" Red asked.

"No," Pete said, "but Frenchy's always willin'."

"Damn you, Pete," Red said, "you know I don't go for that."

"Well, Frenchy sure does," Farris said. "You get in a tight, Red . . ."

Red uttered an obscenity and the two men walked up the little hill and disappeared over the top. Pete stood there, smoking. He lay his rifle down and stood there, looking up at the stars.

So now Zak knew where Leo's men were. A mile away. Evidently the Navajos were in their own camp. It could be right next to Leo's, in fact. But he knew where Leo was, and that gave him hope that he might take out one field commander, perhaps.

The night was turning chill. Cool air blew down from the high peaks and Zak felt it on his face.

Pete would not stay where he was for long, he was sure. He was already stepping up and down in place. Perhaps the cold was seeping up through his boots.

There was no sound from the two men who had left.

Pete finished his cigarette. He threw it down and crushed the butt with the heel of his boot.

Zak held his breath. He would wait a few more minutes.

No, Pete would not stay long.

It was time for him to go.

It was time for him to die.

Zak laid the Henry down. He let the barrel rest in a fork on one of the bushes.

He wiped his sweaty palms on his trousers. One of them became sticky with blood. He wiped the blood off on a different spot.

Pete heard the slight sound.

He reached down and picked up his rifle.

Yes, Pete, Zak thought. Time for you to go.

Time to die.

26

The stars seemed fixed in place, pinholes in a giant swatch of black velvet curtain. Pete Carmody stood like an obsidian obelisk below that backdrop, rifle in hand, his senses as much in the dark as his body.

"Who's there?" he said. Then, in Spanish, "*Quien es?*"

Zak thought that Pete probably thought one of his own sentries had made the sound, and the sentries were mostly Navajo.

"Jorge," Zak answered.

Pete would not be expecting Jorge, but he did not know that he was dead, either.

"Jorge," Pete said. "Ralph with you?"

Zak stood up. His pistol was still in its holster, but his hand floated just above the grip.

"Uh-uh," Zak said.

"Did you rub out Cody?"

"Uh-huh."

"Good. You sound funny. Been sippin' on that mescal, amigo?"

Zak measured the distance between himself and

Carmody. Less than fifteen yards. Maybe twelve. Close enough.

Pete relaxed and lowered his rifle.

When Zak didn't answer, Pete spoke again. "Hell, come on, Jorge. I want to hear all about it. You get Vickers, too? And what about Carlita?"

Zak took a step toward Pete. "Pete," he said, "you see that curtain hanging over your head?"

"What the hell? You ain't Jorge."

"No, Pete. And that rifle better stay where it is. I asked you about the curtain."

"What curtain?"

"Just think of me as a stagehand, Pete." Zak spoke in a low voice. He was very calm.

"What in hell are you talkin' about? That you, Cody?"

"That curtain," Zak said.

"You ain't makin' no sense, Cody."

"Take your last breath, Pete. I'm going to drop the curtain on you."

Pete started to bring his rifle up to his shoulder.

Zak went into a crouch. His hand dove for his pistol like a plummeting bird of prey. The Colt jumped from its holster, smooth and steady like a striking snake. He thumbed the hammer back. The gun came level at his hip, its snout aimed just below Pete's breastbone.

Zak squeezed the trigger and the pistol barked, spat lead and smoke and fire, littering the air with orange lightning bugs. The bullet struck Pete square in his chest. A crimson flower blossomed on his chest and there was the ugly sound of bone cracking and splintering as the soft lead mashed into a fist-shaped mushroom and ripped through flesh and veins before it blew a hole in his back and sent a rosy mist onto the hillside, spattering the rocks with red freckles.

"Ahhh," Pete gasped as the air flew out of his lungs. He staggered backward and looked up at the curtain of sky, saw it come down on him, with all those little pinholes of silver. He fell against the side of the hill, lay splayed there like some ravished mannequin, his rifle still gripped tightly in one hand.

A small plume of smoke curled out of Zak's pistol barrel. He walked over and stood looking down at what was left of Pete.

He could see little stars in Pete's eyes. Blood bubbled up into his mouth and spilled over his lower lip and onto his chin.

"Arrrgh," Pete gasped, unable to form the single curse word that had leaked from his dying mind.

Zak opened the gate to the Colt's cylinder, worked the ejection lever. The empty hull *spanged* against a rock on the ground. Zak worked a fresh cartridge from his belt and replaced the empty shell, closed the gate, spun the cylinder, and eased the hammer down to half cock. He slipped the pistol back in its holster.

A last rasp of air escaped from Pete's throat and his eyes closed as he shuddered one last time.

Zak retrieved the Henry and climbed the little hill. Biederman's camp lay a mile away. The sound of the shot would carry far in the night air. But that far? It depended upon how many hills and rocky outcroppings lay between. He could still feel its reverberations in his ear, then only the rush of air like the sound of the ocean in a seashell.

Zak moved quickly up the hill and into another

world, a world that reeked of its ancient past. There, just beyond the hill, lay a long, wide valley. The moon rose above the rimrock and shone down on the ruins of old adobes. There were canyons formed by towering cliffs, small buttes and mesas. He crossed an old riverbed and trekked through crumbling adobe dwellings, their corners white with thick cobwebs, their roofs washed away by some long-ago flood. He saw shards of old pottery and the bones and skulls of animals—sheep and squirrel and deer. There was a mesa ahead, and he heard horses whickering and smelled their dung. He saw shadowy figures walking guard posts atop the mesa, and below, more adobe dwellings, which seemed to surround it.

In the soft glow of the moon, the mesa looked like an ancient fortress. Zak did not walk close to it, but skirted it at a distance of three hundred yards, skulking through empty adobes, climbing small rock piles. He kept his bearings, reflecting on where Loomis had gone and what he must do to attack such a stronghold.

Zak traveled beyond the low mesa and saw others, and when he climbed to higher ground, he knew where many of the Navajos were, for he saw their small campfires and smelled sheep and horses and mules, saw them on grassy swards in between the mesas and some atop them.

He took one of the canyons that veered off from the valley and strode into silence and deep shadows. He followed its winding track, reduced to miniature by the size of the walls on both sides, and the sheer immensity of a land full of secret hiding places and secret legends long lost to time.

By dead reckoning, Zak figured where Loomis was camped and found a fissure in the rock wall, a game trail behind it, leading up to the rimrock. He marked the position of the stars, figuring by the pole star where he had to go. He was still cautious and made little sound. He walked on sandy and rocky soil mixed in with lava dust and finally reached the rim and took his bearings.

He built a small stone cairn at the top to mark the trail he had taken. He headed east, away from the Navajo camp and the mesa, where, surely, Biederman and his men were occupying the old adobe huts. He could see hazy outlines of white men atop one hill and the forms of Indians on another, and knew there might be more men farther up the valley. Perhaps *many* more. Any army marching up the valley would face a storm of bullets shot from high ground right on top of them. A deadly place, a place soaked in blood from past conflicts, he was sure, and a place sacred to the Navajos, who remembered the stories the old wise men told and perhaps remembered from their childhood that place of safety and ritual.

He walked back to the cairn and then headed west, taking his guidance from the North Star, the pole star. He drifted across lumpy ground flocked with wind-gnarled scrub pines, ocotillo, prickly pear, cholla, juniper, and deadwood turned gray and twisted by the wind and rain and time. It was like walking through a graveyard, for skulls—animal and human—littered the ground here and there, and he came across broken arrows and arrowheads and the stones of war clubs and broken bows, cracked war shields and lances reduced to splinters, jutting from between rocks or lying in sandy swales. There were tattered pieces of tanned leather, some bearing skewed beadwork, others dried up like dead leaves or turned to parchment by the elements.

It took Zak less than an hour to reach the mountain where Loomis had made camp. He passed the place where he and Bullard had looked down upon the Navajo encampment, taking only a quick glance to reassure himself of its location and verifying that Navajos still occupied that place. He was sure that some of those canyons in the big valley were avenues connecting that camp to the others.

All the time he was walking over that desolate moonscape, Zak was figuring strategy. No place was impregnable. Formidable, yes, but the very complexity of the area offered an attacking army concealment and enough places to mount riflemen and cannon that would at least give Loomis a chance to attack and perhaps conquer.

He descended to the big hill and was challenged by an army sentry.

"Who goes there?" a voice called from the shadow of some trees.

"Colonel Zak Cody," he said.

"You come this way real slow, mister."

"I'm not in uniform."

"I know who you are, sir. I got to see your face."

Zak approached, the rifle over his left shoulder.

"Stop right there," the voice commanded.

Zak halted and stood there.

"Corporal of the guard," the man sounded out, and Zak heard running boots on hard ground.

"What is it, Private?"

"Man says he's Colonel Zak Cody. That him there?"

A corporal with a rifle approached. The muzzle was aimed straight at Cody.

"You Colonel Cody?"

"I am."

"Colonel Loomis said you might come from any-wheres. Or out of nowhere. I guess it's you."

"Take me to him immediately," Zak said.

The corporal started to salute, but brought his hand down.

Zak smiled.

Moments later he was sitting in a tent with Jerry Loomis. The flap was open to let in the moonlight.

"Not safe to light a lamp," Loomis said apologetically.

"I don't need to see you, Jerry. And you sure as hell don't want to see me."

"I understand. You reek of death."

"You're in a good spot here," Zak said. "But you're going to have to move. Tonight."

"Again?"

"Yes. And it's going to be rough."

"Are you going to give me a report? I need to know what we're facing."

Zak told him where Biederman was camped with his men and where many of the Navajos were. He left out details of his encounters with both white men and Indians.

"In the morning, I'll draw you a map and show you where you can deploy men and the howitzers on high ground. And I'll show you where you can run cavalry in on those who desert the mesas. If you make it hot enough for them, they'll come down into that valley and you'll find excellent hunting."

"You make it sound like a lark, Zak."

"It's not a lark, Jerry. It's going to be damned bloody, but I think you can tack their hides to the barn door."

"You sound pretty sure of yourself."

"I'll be there, Colonel, scouting for you, like I once did for General Crook."

"That gives me some comfort," Loomis said wryly.

Zak whistled for Nox after he emerged from Loomis's tent, and the horse came running up after a few minutes.

The camp was moving within an hour, following Zak up to the deserted mesa. Loomis had issued orders to his men: no talking, no smoking, no noise.

They made noise, of course, but were fairly quiet. The carts avoided going over large stones, and the men guiding the howitzers were careful to stay away from rocky stretches and to stop often to breathe the mules.

Vickers and Bullard caught up with Zak two hours into the march.

"I brung your hat, Zak," Bullard said, handing the black hat over to him. "Case you need it."

Zak put the hat on over his headband, squared it off at a jaunty tilt.

"Zak," Vickers said, "you've got blood all over you. You get into a fight?"

"This is old blood," Zak said. "Tomorrow I'll get a fresh coat. And so will you and Randy."

They rode across that empty land of bones and

weapons, the moon spraying them with a ghostly light, their shadows rippling like wrinkles on an old man's bare hide. The snowcapped mountains in the distance looked like the heads of bald eagles, wise and silent as the stars above them.

27

The tent walls shivered in the wind. Candlelight threw skulking shadows on the ground and scrawled them on the white fabric. Men huddled around Zak, who, with his knife, was drawing a series of squares and circles into the dirt. The tent made a sound like a ship's sail flapping in a stiff breeze. Colonel Loomis chewed on an unlit cigar. Captain Jubal Hazard, a dwarfish man with a craggy face and full beard, squatted like a gnome, his tiny blue eyes crackling like star sapphires as he breathed out sour whiskey fumes mixed with the scent from a cinnamon stick.

Vickers and Bullard watched the knife cut deep and score trails and lines that represented two sides of a valley.

"Captain Hazard," Zak said, "you won't be able to cover the field with your howitzers. You'll place one here and the other, here. Mostly, they will be used to cause confusion and repel any Navajo brave enough to climb up after you."

"You show me the spots, I'll set 'em," Hazard said.

"Jeff, you'll take a dozen troops and ride down

to this end of the valley. Colonel Loomis, you'll split your remaining forces into two groups, one to lay down fire on this mesa, the other to rake that one with rifle fire. Then you'll draw them together at this point and form into a circle. You'll have targets at every point on that circle."

"What are you going to do, Zak?" Loomis asked.

"Sergeant Bullard and I are going on a special mission. First, we'll sneak up into Biederman's camp and slay his fat ass, if we can, and anyone who gets in our way or crosses our sights."

"Pretty risky."

"Jerry, down in that flat, breathing is risky," Zak said.

"And then what?" Vickers asked.

"I want to draw Narbona out. I think he's on this other mesa. I figure he'll stand out from the rest of the Navajos and might be with his man, Largos. If I can, I want to blow both their lamps out. Pop, pop." Zak made a pistol with the thumb and forefinger of his right hand.

Nobody laughed.

"Seems to me you're taking the most risks," Loomis said, cradling his chin in the palm of his left hand and working his cigar to the other side of his mouth.

"Sergeant Bullard is going to watch my back. I'm going up to the Biederman mesa decked out like a Navajo. But I'll be a shadow. When you hear the first shot, Captain Hazard, you'll start lobbing cannonballs onto the Narbona mesa. Colonel, I want some of your men on this shelf right above the Biederman mesa. When they see men running out of those adobe lodges, they should fire at will."

Zak drew a large *B* in the center of one circle, and a large *N* in the other.

"I figure there are more Navajos up those canyons. When they come out into the valley, Colonel, your two groups will be able to drop them before they can do any damage. So, you'll have plenty of shooting to do. Both mesas, the valley, and any who come riding out of those canyons."

"Any idea of how many we're facing?" Loomis asked, his forehead knitted into deep furrows of flesh.

"You'll probably be outnumbered. But you'll have the advantage. If I can cut off the heads of Narbona and Biederman, their men may run around like chickens with their heads cut off."

"That's a lot of cutting," Vickers said, trying to be cheerful.

"It's going to be a butcher shop down there," Zak said. "You'll all be lopping off heads, legs, arms, and maybe a few balls."

Everyone laughed except Loomis.

Later, Zak erased his map and blew out the candle. He took Hazard to the edge of the flat mountain and showed him where to place his two cannons.

"Can't see much in this dark," Hazard said.

"You will when it gets light. I'll show you your aiming points to start you off. You just have your men set and ready to load powder and ball."

"Yes, sir," Hazard said, and he waddled after Zak over the ground where he would set his howitzers as Zak blazed the small trees that marked boundaries and positions.

Zak showed Loomis the defile where he would send his troops, and just before dawn, he wished him luck.

He met with Vickers and Bullard near where all the horses were gathered. He took off his hat and gave it to Bullard.

"Tie this to my saddle, Randy," he said. "And where'd you put my boots?"

"In one of your saddlebags, Zak."

"And what did you do with that Henry I gave you?"

"I stored it with my kit. A souvenir, unless you want it."

"No. You and Captain Vickers take your carbines. I'm just going to carry my pistol and my knife."

"You sure you know what you're doing, Zak?" Jeff asked.

"Right now, I'm going over my part in my mind. It's like cards."

"Like cards?"

"If you're a good gambler, you play the game before you even get to the table. You deal every hand, play every ace, draw every hole card, place every bet."

"What good does that do?" Randy asked, scratching his head.

"It helps to eliminate any surprises."

Zak shook hands with Vickers and wished him luck.

Then, in the darkness before dawn, he and Bullard set off down the trail to the valley.

"Don't talk to me, Randy," Zak warned him as they started down the defile. "If you need to say something, tap me on the shoulder and use hand signals. Can you do that?"

"Sure," Randy said, swallowing a lump of air.

"Let's go."

"One, thing, Zak. You goin' to kill Biederman. Right?"

"That's right."

"What about his wife? Minnie."

"You want to kill her?"

"Well, no, sir. I mean, she's a woman and all."

"She's the enemy, Randy. Blood sister to Narbona."

"You'd shoot a woman?"

"I would this one. Come on."

The two men stole into the valley. Bullard matched Zak step for step and stopped when he stopped, listened when he listened. They got to the Biederman mesa without being detected. In the predawn darkness, Zak found the trail up to the top. He saw men walking guard duty, shadowy silhouettes with no definition, no personalities. They might as well have been scarecrows, as far as he was concerned. A stiff breeze blew down the wide canyon and chilled them to the bone.

"When we get up there, you lay low. Just watch my back. Shoot anyone who comes up behind me. But I'm going to use my knife, so you probably won't have to use your rifle. Once that first shot is fired, all hell's going to break loose."

There were only two men walking the camp's perimeter. Zak motioned for Bullard to lie flat and wait.

It was still dark, but the stars told him that dawn was not far away.

Zak huddled next to the nearest adobe and waited for the guard on his side to walk past him.

The sky seemed to grow darker.

It's true, then, he thought. It's always darkest before the dawn.

And it was also the most dangerous time, he knew.

The guard walked past where Bullard was lying flat. Zak watched him. He didn't see the sergeant.

He drew his knife to play his hand of cards before the guard came to his table. Zak knew just what to do and how to do it.

He heard a man snoring. Another hawked up a gob of phlegm in one of the adobes.

He listened to the men inside the adobe next to him. Their breathing was like a sighing wind, even and steady. Dead to the world, he thought. Wasn't that what mothers said about their children when they were fast asleep?

He drew his knife.

Dead to the world.

Almost.

⊷ 28 ⊷

Zak rose up and struck with the ferocity of a panther. He strapped one arm around the man's head, clamping his mouth shut, then sliced across the neck just above the collarbone. The man struggled for just a moment, then slumped into Zak's arms as blood spurted from his cut throat. Zak laid him gently down, put a moccasined foot on his chest, and pressed hard. If the man had any breath left in his lungs, Zak squeezed it out, right then and there.

Zak dragged the dead man over next to the adobe. He took off the man's hat and put it on. He picked up his rifle, a Sharps carbine, and took up the guard's walk where he had left off. He would meet the other one a hundred or so yards from where he was.

He heard noise above, up in the brush, and the faint sound of cartwheels buzzing on sandy soil and thumping occasionally on rocky ground. Over on the Narbona mesa, he saw flickers of cook fires and, on the breeze, he smelled the aroma of fried bread. The Navajos had been making it ever since Kit Carson had taken some to Bosque Redondo and the army had given them flour and salt for subsistence. The smell made his stomach roil with hunger, but he walked the walk, just the way the guard he'd killed had done it, and when he met the other man, he saw his face change. He could not see his expression, but he imagined that his eyebrows arched and his mouth dropped open.

Just for an instant.

Zak closed on him and stuck the barrel of the Sharps in the man's gut.

"You keep your mouth shut," Zak whispered, "and just point to the 'dobe where Leo and Minnie are sleeping."

When the man raised his arm, Zak jerked his rifle from his shoulder. The man pointed to an adobe about thirty yards away.

"How many in there with Leo? Just hold up your fingers. If just Leo and Minnie are there, hold up two. If more, you give me the count."

The man held up two fingers. Zak could feel him shaking against the muzzle of the rifle. He, like the others of Leo's band, had a tied-down holster. Zak slipped the pistol from the scabbard and pointed to the shadows next to an adobe.

The man turned and walked toward the dark place where he would die.

Zak wasted no time. He shoved the pistol in his belt, laid the two rifles down, and throttled the man. Then he jabbed his knife straight into his throat, just below his Adam's apple, twisting the blade to widen the wound. The man made a low gurgle in his throat, doubled over, and Zak eased him to the ground. The gushing blood sounded like running water for just a moment and left a shiny pool on the ground, its center filled with the reflections of a half dozen dazzling stars.

Zak looked up at the sky and to the east. The sky was paling beyond the Jemez, the stars fading like autumn flowers.

He crept into the adobe with its open, glassless windows. He hugged the wall inside and listened to the breathing of the two people. There was no hurry now. He shrank into the darkest corner, wiped the blade of his knife on his trousers and slipped it back into its sheath. It made a faint whisper. Zak held his breath.

Neither of the two sleepers stirred, and he let his breath ease out slowly through his nostrils.

Pale light began to seep through the open windows. Zak looked at the two lumps on the bedrolls, a single blanket covering man and wife.

He could smell the musk of Minnie, the sweat and whiskey on the breath of Leo. He listened for any outside sounds, and smelled the fried bread wafting on the breeze that still blew down from the high mountains.

Leo made a sound in his throat. He threw an arm over the blanket, held on to it for a moment, then let go. Zak wondered if Leo had a pistol lying next to him. He was pretty sure that Minnie had a knife either strapped to her leg or in her sash.

He could see them better now. Minnie slept with her mouth closed. Leo's mouth was open.

They were dead to the world, he thought, and tried not to smile.

It was getting lighter outside. He did not have much time.

He walked to the other side of room, away from

the doorway and the windows. He stood on the side where Leo slept, not four feet away.

"Biederman," Zak said softly. "Leo."

"Whuh?" Biederman looked around with sleepy eyes. He started to rise from his bedroll. "Who's 'at?" he mumbled.

Minnie made a sound, but she was still asleep. She moaned. It was a kind of whining moan, Zak thought.

"I'm the drummer," Zak said to Leo.

"What drummer? I didn't order no goods."

Leo rose up to a sitting position, suddenly wide awake. He squinted at Zak, trying to make out who he was.

"I've got your order right here, Mr. Biederman. Remember? You ordered it in Santa Fe."

"I didn't order nothin' from no drummer."

"Yes, you did. I have it for you."

"God damn it, what the hell is it?"

"Death," Zak said.

Biederman lunged for his pistol, which was still in its holster by his bedroll.

Zak filled his hand with blued iron and wood and thumbed the hammer back. Just as Leo's fingers touched the grip of his pistol, Zak fired, aiming right at the center of Biederman's forehead. The explosion boomed in the confines of the adobe and Minnie boiled out of her bedding like a flushed prairie chicken. She came up with a blade in her hand. Acrid smoke filled the room and she screamed as she whirled and came charging straight at Zak, her arm raised, the knife poised like the head of a striking cobra.

She cursed him in Navajo.

"I don't understand your language," Zak said, and shot her in the heart. He stepped aside as her momentum carried her straight to him. She crumpled into the wall, bleeding through the hole in her chest, her pumping heart in its last wild throes.

Zak didn't wait to watch her die. He slipped out of the adobe and ran to where Bullard was waiting.

"Let's go," he said.

Bullard ran at breakneck speed down the trail to the top of the mesa, Zak right behind him.

A pale light glowed in the east. Most of the stars had vanished, and a color like the violet in a morning glory was spreading westward. The white peaks shone as each snow crystal caught the rising sun and threw up an aura that was like an alabaster mist.

Zak guided Bullard to cover and they squatted behind rocks as the top of the mesa rang with the shouts of men awakened suddenly from their sleep.

"God, those shots sounded so damned loud," Bullard whispered.

"Just wait until Hazard opens up with those cannons."

"Who'd you get, Zak? Biederman?"

"And Minnie."

"Lord."

"No, not him, Randy. He's still with us."

"How can you make a joke at a time like this? We've got to get the hell out of here."

"If you see anyone come down that trail, Randy, you shoot whoever it is."

"It's not light enough."

Zak ejected the empty shells, stuffed two more cartridges into his Colt. "Any minute now," he said.

"Any minute what?" Randy asked.

"Captain Hazard will start his music."

A man came to the edge of the mesa and looked down at the valley. He saw nothing, so he ran back, and there was more shouting and angry yells as some of Biederman's men discovered the dead bodies.

Then the golden rim of the sun cleared the distant horizon, lighting clouds shaped like long loaves of bread, turning them pink and lavender and spraying light through them until they radiated like the stained-glass windows in a church.

Thunder rocked the morning as the howitzers opened up, and Zak saw a ball strike the Narbona mesa, exploding in a cloud of smoke.

Then the second round hit, and men screamed as the explosion tore away their limbs and smashed their bodies to pulp.

"Time to go," Zak said to Bullard.

"Where we goin'?"

"I want to see if I can kill a ghost warrior, Randy."

"Huh?"

"Narbona," Zak said and started running toward the base of the mesa.

Rifles crackled and there was the acrid smell of cordite in the air. Smoke drifted toward them, broke up into wisps above their heads.

Barebacked horses streamed into the valley from a nearby canyon, driven by mounted Navajos waving blankets. Men poured from the tops of both mesas, racing down the trails. The saddled horses emerged from another canyon, white men driving them as if on cue.

Zak raced on, looking at every Navajo brave, looking for one man among many.

Narbona.

≈ 29 ≈

Cavalry troops surged into the valley. Rifle fire erupted like a string of Chinese firecrackers. Troops surrounded the two mesas. Some closed with the Navajo horsemen, engaging them in battle. Smoke streamed in every direction, sometimes blossoming into clouds. There was the acrid stench of exploded gunpowder.

Men screamed and fell from their horses, on both sides. Officers yelled orders; some men roared in the rage of the battle, while others carried out their lethal duties with utter silence and determination.

Zak and Randy wove their way through crashing horses and men rushing to their mounts, ducking under a hail of bullets that buzzed over their heads like wingless leaden hornets.

The Navajos swarmed and dispersed, only to dash in and out of lines of mounted troops. The troops cleared paths that closed up behind them, formed new attack routes, until the entire melee was a freeform brawl of mounted men dashing after enemies on every side.

Zak scanned the Navajo horsemen, looking for any that stood out, watching for a leader and his followers. He and Randy reached the Narbona mesa and ran up the path to the top, encountering no resistance.

Zak thought, Where does an animal go when it has reached the point of desperation? It climbs the highest tree, it seeks out the deepest cave, it makes its last stand in a place of safety, a place where it feels at home.

They looked at the dome-shaped hogans, all facing east, scattered like beehives atop the mesa.

"Check every one, Randy," Zak said. "Shoot anything that moves."

Zak ran among the adobe hovels, entered a circle, and spotted a single dwelling in the center.

He halted a few yards from it, standing to one side in case anyone was inside.

"Ho, Narbona," he called. Then, in Spanish, he said: "*Yo soy Dinéh. Vengo con un mensaje por un hombre quien se llama Narbona. Narbona, un cobarde, la basura de la tierra.*"

"I am Navajo. I come with a message for a man who calls himself Narbona. Narbona, a coward, the filth of the earth."

He heard muffled voices from inside the hogan. A man appeared at the entrance, a rifle in his hands. His face was painted, smeared with signs and symbols, streaks of vermillion, circles of yellow and white, vermicular scrawls of black. The man saw Zak and raised his rifle to his shoulder.

"Largos," Zak called, his hand streaking for his pistol.

Largos hesitated, surprised at hearing his name.

"You were with the dead and now you return," Zak said in Spanish.

Largos scowled, his face becoming a pinched mass of painted bronze. Zak fired his pistol as the man seated the butt of his rifle in the hollow of his shoulder. The bullet smashed him high in the left part of his chest. His mouth went slack and his eyes widened in surprise. Zak shot him again as he pitched forward, slumped to the ground.

Another man appeared in the doorway. His face and body were painted white and there were black circles around his eyes, red streaks at the corners of his mouth. He wore only a breechclout and moccasins.

"Narbona," Zak said, still speaking in Spanish, "you stole the name of a brave warrior. He sent me to bring back his name."

"*Quien eres tu?*" Narbona asked, reaching for the pistol hanging from his belt.

"I am the horseman of the shadow," Zak said.

"So, you are Shadow Rider. Where do you come from?"

"I come from the land of the dead. Narbona wants his name returned to him. The name you stole."

"I am Narbona."

"You are a ghost," Zak said, and the Colt bucked in his hand, smoke and flame spouting from its blue-black muzzle. Narbona raised his pistol. The bullet smashed into his face, ripping off his nose and the lower part of his brain. His forehead collapsed inward and a rosy spray of blood shot out of his left temple as splinters of bone exploded into the door jamb. The man's legs folded beneath him and he settled in a heap, one eye staring at the blue sky, the other pooched out like a boiled egg, riddled with streaks of blood.

The dead man had no face.

"And, now," Zak said softly, as he opened the gate of his Colt and began ejecting the empty hulls, "you have no name."

He reloaded his pistol and put it back in its holster. He dragged Narbona's body to the edge of the mesa. He put his hands in his armpits and held him up, shook his body back and forth. Then he threw him over the side, watched his body tumble and crash on the rocks below, where all could see.

Randy met him as Zak walked back through the hogans.

"Colonel Loomis has got 'em on the run, Zak."

Zak said nothing. He wondered how Jeff Vickers had fared.

When he descended from the mesa, he had his answer. Vickers was holding Nox and a horse for Bullard. He had Zak's crumpled hat in his hand.

"I see you got a fresh coat of blood, Zak," Jeff said.

Zak climbed into the saddle and heaved with a heavy intake of breath.

"And you're still out of uniform, Captain."

"You got Narbona. When the Navajos saw him fall from the mesa, they cut and run."

"I didn't get Narbona, Jeff. Narbona died a long time ago."

And now, he thought, Narbona's ghost could rest, at last.